THUNDERWOOD

BY
GARY BARGATZE

Warfield
Happy Hollow
Hurricane Creek
Hollow Rock
McGill
Cabedelo

**Upcoming Titles in the
Your Winding Daybreak Ways Series**

Babylon, A Human Requiem

THUNDERWOOD

GARY BARGATZE

RIGOR HILL PRESS

For Jim and Patty, who know

Ax. 1. $\{P(\varphi) \wedge \Box\, \forall x[\varphi(x) \to \psi(x)]\} \to P(\psi)$

Ax. 2. $P(\neg\varphi) \leftrightarrow \neg P(\varphi)$

Th. 1. $P(\varphi) \to \Diamond\, \exists x[\varphi(x)]$

Df. 1. $G(x) \iff \forall\varphi[P(\varphi) \to \varphi(x)]$

Ax. 3. $P(G)$

Th. 2. $\Diamond\, \exists x\, G(x)$

Df. 2. $\varphi \text{ ess } x \iff \varphi(x) \wedge \forall\psi\, \{\psi(x) \to \Box\, \forall y[\varphi(y) \to \psi(y)]\}$

Ax. 4. $P(\varphi) \to \Box\, P(\varphi)$

Th. 3. $G(x) \to G \text{ ess } x$

Df. 3. $E(x) \iff \forall\varphi[\varphi \text{ ess } x \to \Box\, \exists y\, \varphi(y)]$

Ax. 5. $P(E)$

Th. 4. $\Box\, \exists x\, G(x)$

01000001011100110010000001110100 0110
1000011001010010000000100110001101111
0111001001100100001000000110001101101
1110110110101101101011000010110111001
1001000110010101100100001000000100110
1011011110111001101100101011100110010
1100001000000111001101101111001000000
1101000011001010010000001101110011101
0101101101011000100110010101110010011
0010101100100001000000111010001101000
0110010101101101001000000110100101101
1100010000001110100011010000110010100
1000000111011101101001011011000110010
0011001010111001001101110011001010111
001101110011

Numbers 1:19

1

THE WHISPERERS SAID I am what I am because the gods punished my parents for their incestuous love. But punished them with my loneliness? My awkwardness? My emotional deafness? My obsessions? My compulsions? My outbursts? My fears? My unending quest for acceptance? My unanswered prayers for deliverance? My refuge in motherboards? My lifetime longing to be someone other than me?

Early on, the insidious cycle of confusion, action, and reaction began corralling and driving my dreams up the narrowing ramp one by one toward the slaughter pen. But to my parents' credit I recall now how hard they fought to move the authorities past "fixing me" to acknowledging their own blindness when dealing with my differences.

"Come on in," the man said, smiling and extending his hand. "I'm Bob Sussman, the new principal here at McGill Elementary."

"Sam Lynch, sir. Jason's father."

"And you must be Jason's mother, Mrs. Lynch," the principal interjected as he shook Mama's hand.

"Yes, Mr. Sussman, I'm Jason's mother, but the name's de Silva. Danielle de Silva."

"Sorry, ah, Ms. de Silva," Principal Sussman said, his embarrassment coloring his cheeks. "I… I just assumed."

Mama interrupted politely. "No problem, Mr. Sussman. It's not the first time."

He quickly turned and introduced two middle-aged women. "This is, ah, Mrs. Summerfield, Jason's fifth-grade teacher, and, ah, this is our school psychologist, Dr. Goodyear."

"Nice to meet y'all," my father responded.

The principal motioned toward the far side of the table and said, "Mr. and Mrs.—ah, Ms. de Silva—the two of you and Jason take a seat over there, and let's get started." He paused until everyone was seated and then continued in a more serious, businesslike tone. "You know why we've asked you to come in early this morning for a conference?"

My father nodded. "According to your note, you want to discuss Jason's progress and behavior."

"Yes. Yes. So first of all let me speak for the three of us here on staff. Jason's a very bright boy with a great deal of potential. It's our opinion, however, that he… he just doesn't apply himself. He seems to be dreaming all the time, in another world, unless we're talking about computers, geology, or shipwrecks."

Dr. Goodyear jumped in. "Of course, this isn't anything new… as y'all know from the feedback the teachers have been providing over the past couple of years on his report cards."

"You mean the comments like 'daydreamer,' 'lazy,' 'off task'?" Mama asked coolly.

"His third- and fourth-grade teachers might have been a bit blunt in their assessments," Dr. Goodyear responded, "but

2

it's been an ongoing issue. I mean, not finishing his homework and classroom work on time."

My father interrupted politely. "I don't think it's because he's not trying. I believe his second-grade teacher put her finger on at least part of the problem. She suggested he needed help getting his thoughts and work organized. And for our part we got right on it. We hired a tutor to work with Jason on his organizational skills. He's shown some improvement, but for the most part, it's been slow going. And despite his good performance on standardized tests, Danielle and I know he still struggles with his schoolwork. But I don't think it's because he's 'lazy' or a 'daydreamer.' I think it's a struggle getting his thoughts organized in his mind and then getting them down on paper."

Mrs. Summerfield turned to the psychologist and said, "Perhaps the special ed teacher could work with Jason one-on-one. She has a good rapport with all the children. But any ideas how she could help with his organizational skills?"

Dr. Goodyear nodded. "We can take this offline, Betty, but the short answer's yes. Jennifer Davis could work with Jason on making lists, visual schedules, daily planners. Give him tips on how to set goals, manage projects, remember details. Help him organize and plan his assignments."

Principal Sussman looked across the table at the three of us and said, "Sounds like a plan to me. You folks comfortable with Dr. Goodyear's suggestions?"

My mother responded appreciatively, "There's no harm in trying. And please keep us posted on what we can be doing at home to reinforce your training here at school."

After an awkward silence, Mr. Sussman cleared his throat and said, "I guess we should talk about the bigger elephant in the room—Jason's odd, ah, *unusual* behavior. So, Mrs. Summerfield, you want to start?"

The teacher looked down at her notes uncomfortably and began reading. "Ah, Jason seems to want to spend a lot of time alone in the classroom and on the playground. When we're outside, he doesn't want to participate in games or interact with his classmates."

My mother leaned forward and interjected, "He's afraid!"

"Afraid?" Mr. Sussman asked.

"Yes, afraid. There's not a week goes by he doesn't come home crying. I've even found him standing at my vanity wearing my blouses and smearing makeup and lipstick all around. When I've asked Jason to explain himself, he says he would rather be someone else—maybe even a girl like me."

"But afraid? Afraid of what?" Dr. Goodyear asked.

My father weighed in. "That... that bully. The sociopath. The alderman's son. Jason says the boy punches him, smacks his glasses off his face and..."

My mother grabbed my father's arm. "Sam, please... please."

Mrs. Summerfield shook her head and responded defensively, "I've never seen anything of the sort on the playground. Perhaps Jason is exaggerating."

My father blurted sarcastically, "Do you think the kid's gonna do anything to Jason while you're watching him? Let's not be naïve, Mrs. Summerfield."

Dr. Goodyear stepped in trying to calm the waters. "If we'd known of your concerns, Mr. Lynch, we would have been on the lookout for any misbehavior on Robby's part. But rest assured we'll be keeping an eye on it from now on."

"I'm sorry for the outburst," my father said. "But I've… I've always hated it when bigger people beat up on smaller folk. It's just my nature to rail against injustice—and especially when it's my own flesh and blood."

Mr. Sussman responded, "We understand where you're coming from, Mr. Lynch. I'm sure the three of us here would all feel the same way." He paused briefly to collect his thoughts and then continued. "Let's move on now to Jason's classroom behavior. Mrs. Summerfield, you want to give Ms. de Silva and Mr. Lynch some examples of Jason's conduct during class?"

The fifth-grade teacher nodded and consulted her notes. "Jason can be impulsive," she said, looking from one parent to the other. "Abrupt at times. Two weeks into the semester I was leading a discussion of Jules Verne's *Journey to the Center of the Earth* and had gotten to the chapters describing the descent into the Icelandic crater. And when Professor Lidenbrock reached an enormous cavern filled with a subterranean ocean, Jason jumped up and shouted, 'That's stupid! The lithosphere is solid rock, and when you get below the crust and upper mantle at the fifty- to sixty-mile mark, when you get into the asthenosphere, you begin dealing with temperatures that turn rock to Jell-O. According to the geothermal gradient—one degree Fahrenheit per seventy feet of depth—that's almost three thousand degrees! And the professor's gonna survive that? No way! That's just stupid!'

"I tried stopping him several times, but he was off to the races. He wouldn't sit down for anything. And once he relates our classroom discussion to one of his obsess— Ah, interests—computers, shipwrecks, geology and the like—there's no stopping him."

Dr. Goodyear jumped in with her diagnosis. "Perseveration."

"Preserve… ?" Mama asked.

"Perseveration. In layman's terms it's going off the deep end, going on and on about something."

Now it was Mama's turn to get riled up. "With all due respect, Dr. Goodyear, I think you're turning one of Jason's strengths into a weakness. From an early age he could focus on a subject and retain the tiniest details. But you've taken his gift and turned it inside out. Turned it into a monster. Into psychobabble. Calling his behavior 'pers… perseveration.' But where I come from, 'persevering' is a positive trait. All of you here at the school are only focusing on the negative."

"But it's disruptive," Mrs. Summerfield shot back. "It's unfair to his classmates. Makes Jason stand out… and not in a good way."

"We'll give you that, Mrs. Summerfield," Father said, playing peacemaker. "Jason's out-of-the-box behavior can be trying. We see it around the house sometimes. But let me ask you this. How often does he jump up in class and 'go off to the races,' as you say?"

"Well, let's see. I'd say maybe once or twice a month."

"And other than those one or two occasions a month, he behaves as the rest of the children?"

"Physically? Yes. But mentally, as we explained, he's disengaged much of the time."

Father pushed back. "You think there's a way to cut him some slack here, Mrs. Summerfield? Appreciate the knowledge he's accumulated in such a short time. Perhaps explain to the children Jason sees things differently. Sees them in black and white. No in betweens. Maybe explain how he loves talking about things that interest him. And how he thinks everyone else feels the way he does about computers, shipwrecks, and geology. How he studies a topic for hours on end determined to drill down into the subject as far as he can go."

Mr. Sussman turned to Mrs. Summerfield. "What do you think? Give it a shot?"

"I'll try, sir."

"That's all we can ask of anybody, Betty." The principal then consulted his notes and asked the teacher, "Any other behaviors we need to discuss with Jason's parents this morning?"

Mrs. Summerfield scanned her folder before answering. "Yes, sir. I have several more issues, which I think are a bit more worrisome. Ah, just yesterday—" She paused and turned to Mr. Sussman. "Bob, I haven't had a chance to speak with you yet about this since you were in meetings all day yesterday with the superintendent. But I was walking up and down the rows between the children's desks administering their weekly spelling test, and as I passed Jason's desk, I noticed he hadn't written down any of the words. Instead, he was sketching a man with a large knife and a rifle. I kneeled down and whispered, 'What's this? What are you doing?' Jason looked up but didn't say anything. He just sat there staring at me with the most defiant grin you'll ever see." She shook her head and concluded, "The combination of the drawing and that grin unnerved me a bit. And this was on top of the Halloween outfit where he showed up armed with a battle-axe!"

My father leaned in. I could tell he was steaming. But to his credit he kept his cool this time. "Let's just agree up front, Mrs. Summerfield, that Jason should've been taking his test rather than drawing. But did you ever ask him who the man was in the picture?"

She shrugged and replied, "No. I assumed he was sketching himself."

My father turned to me and asked, "Jason, who was the man in the drawing?"

"Davy Crockett."

"Where was Davy, son?"

"In Texas at the Alamo."

"Ya see, Mrs. Summerfield, we'd just finished watching the 1960 John Wayne movie *The Alamo*."

"But why'd Jason smile then when I asked him what he was up to?"

Mama leaned forward and asked Dr. Goodyear, "You ever come across this in your training?"

"Come across what, Ms. de Silva?"

"Come across a plausible explanation for why Jason might have been smiling?"

8

"Can't say that I have. I would only be guessing."

"Well, there was nothing sinister about the drawing or the smile, Mrs. Summerfield. Jason's a visual learner. When we find a movie or a documentary that fairly accurately describes a historical event, we like to sit down as a family and watch the film. And then afterwards, we'll reinforce the facts with a follow-up discussion.

"As for the grin, it's counterintuitive. It took Sam and me a while to figure it out. But in talking to other parents dealing with similar issues we learned kids like Jason smile when they are questioned, when they feel they're under stress. Ya see, Jason didn't mean any harm. He knew he should've been taking the test, and you caught him red-handed.

"And as far as the Halloween outfit goes, Sam and I have to plead guilty there too. We helped Jason make the cloth armor and the wooden battle-axe. You see, Sam and I are in the music business, and during a vacation trip to New York last summer, we took Jason to see the Broadway revival of *Camelot*. We saw the play as an opportunity for a twofer—exposing him to some exceptional stage music and introducing him to the history of King Arthur and the knights of the round table. And believe it or not, some of it must have stuck. We'll hear Jason humming and singing some of the lyrics while he's working on his model medieval castle.

"I'm sorry you became so concerned, Mrs. Summerfield, but believe me, Jason doesn't have a violent streak in him. We've taught him the golden rule: treat people the way you want to be treated. The only problem Sam and I have is trying

9

to explain away his perception that other children don't abide by the same rule."

Mr. Sussman looked down at his watch and said, "We're gonna have to be wrapping up soon. Classes will be starting in fifteen minutes. You have anything else for Jason's parents, Betty?"

"Yes, just one more thing. I don't want this to escalate. To get out of hand."

"What's that, Betty?" Mr. Sussman asked.

"For a week now Jason's been bringing in small bouquets of wildflowers for his classmate, Maggie Bauer. She sits next to him in class. Well, the first time he did it, my aide, Jennifer, and I thought it was a really sweet thing to do. You know, young love and all that. But as I said, Jason's kept it up now going on a week. And poor little Maggie doesn't know what to do. She gets embarrassed, turns red. And I'm sure her classmates have already begun teasing her." Mrs. Summerfield paused, looked across the table at my parents and me, and asked, "Y'all have any idea what Jason's up to here? Why he's started bringing the bouquets in every day?"

My mother nodded and replied, "Yes, I think I can help you out there. Several times this week I saw Jason picking wildflowers along the driveway running up to the house. I asked him what he planned on doing with them. But, ah— On second thought, instead of my explaining, why not let Jason speak for himself?" My mother turned to me and said, "So, Jason, tell Mrs. Summerfield what you told me about the flowers. Tell her why you kept bringing the bouquets in to school every day."

I turned to my mother and said, "Because Maggie has looked so sad."

"You see, Mrs. Summerfield, Jason has a hard time reading faces, understanding people's emotions. What you see as Maggie's chagrin, Jason interprets as sadness. He was simply trying to cheer her up. But rest assured I'll do my best from now on to explain the difference between well-intended and misguided gestures."

Mr. Sussman asked, "Anything else now? Anyone? Well, okay then. I believe we've got a good plan going forward. Our special ed teacher will work one-on-one with Jason. Mrs. Summerfield will try to foster a better understanding of Jason's behavior among his classmates. Our team will try to better communicate the strategies we're working on with him here at school. And y'all will work with him at home reinforcing what we're trying to do here. Does that pretty much sum it up?"

After everyone nodded agreement, Mr. Sussman stood up, signaling the meeting was adjourned. As he extended his hand to my mother, he said, "I want to thank y'all for coming in so early before classes begin. If you have any questions or concerns about anything, please don't hesitate to give us a call." He glanced down at me, tousled my hair, and added, "Our team here wants to do all we can to ensure Jason's success."

My father extended his hand and said, "We know y'all are giving it your best shot."

Mr. Sussman shook my father's hand heartily. "Thank you, Mr. Lynch, for saying that." He then turned to Dr. Goodyear.

"Ah, Millie, would you mind a favor—escorting Ms. de Silva and Mr. Lynch out to the reception area?"

"No problem, Bob."

The principal looked down at me again and said, "And, Jason, you and Mrs. Summerfield make a beeline for class now. Y'all don't want to be late."

"Yes, sir," I replied, sighing and lowering my head.

But after stepping out into the hallway, I stopped to watch my parents and Dr. Goodyear disappear at the far end of the corridor. A crushing loneliness swept over me. My advocates were leaving as I was being forced back into my cell.

2

THE NEUROTYPICAL INTOLERANCE AND occasional abuse we had suffered in fifth grade had intensified over the intervening two years and pushed us solidly into the social backwaters of McGill Junior High. We had all spent the early years of our lives trying to prove ourselves, striving to be as good as our classmates, and playing a lot of roles hoping to fit in, get by, and pass for normal. But strong undercurrents of middle school conformity had inexorably driven us "fucking weirdos" out of the mainstream into the far reaches of the cafeteria at lunchtime and the girls' gymnasium after school, where our social club for the misbegotten held court on the first and third Tuesdays of every month.

Before moving away to Nashville, Carl, a charter member of our group, had conjured up several potential names for the club. Since he had an obsessive interest in cowboy fiction and film, all his suggestions had a western bent to them—The Misfits, The Outlaws, and The Outcasts of Poker Flats. After much handwringing, both literally and figuratively, we decided to go with The Outcasts. Besides having a nice ring to it, The Outcasts of Poker Flats pretty well summed us up and—we hoped—projected a proud, defiant message to the rest of our classmates.

During the lengthy deliberations, Carl emphasized an additional benefit of settling on The Outcasts. There were eight of us, all told, in the club—five boys and three girls—which fortuitously coincided with the total number of characters named in Harte's short story. Since no one ever asked Carl his reasoning, we never knew exactly how he assigned us our names—how he became "Simson," Sandra was "the Duchess," Kevin was "Uncle Billy," Brenda became "Piney Woods," Jeffrey was "Wheeler," Jane was "Mother Shipton," Ethan became "Woods," and I was "Oakhurst."

Following a lot of rank speculation on my part, the only names I would have placed a bet on were Jeffrey assuming the moniker "Wheeler" and Ethan the name "Woods." Since Jeffrey was a paraplegic, it would be a safe bet that Carl chose the name "Wheeler" because of Jeffrey's mode of transportation, his battery-powered wheelchair. Ethan as "Woods" is a slightly riskier proposition; but I would still place a fairly sizable bet on the rationale behind Ethan's christening. You see, Jake Woods is Piney Woods's father; and while Jake is mentioned in Harte's story, he doesn't appear or play an active role in it. He simply hovers somewhere outside the text. And since Ethan's hyperactivity compelled him to jump in and out of our meetings without much of a contribution—now you see him and now you don't—it was easy to make the leap from Ethan to the phantom "Woods."

While the club's official name remained the same after Carl left town, our nicknames morphed over time from those based on Harte's characters to more personal pet names based on either our unique behaviors or our consuming interests at the time. Jeffrey's wheelchair acrobatics earned him the name "Spokes." Jane's obsessive-compulsive behavior engendered the handle "Checkers." Ethan's flitting about led to "Casper." Sandra's obsessive focus on anatomy gave rise to "Bones." Kevin's strong interest in baseball trivia earned him "Stats." Brenda's obsession with African dictators led to "Zulu." And because of my preoccupation with defunct railroads I became "Casey J."

The absurdist playwright Ionesco would have felt right at home. Chaos and non sequiturs reigned supreme during our initial meetings. Everyone talked and no one listened until our guidance counselor, Mrs. Prescott, suggested a way out of the hurly-burly. Since many of us were consumed by our obsessive interests, why not have only one speaker per meeting on a rotating basis; allow that classmate to wax eloquent on his or her favorite topic; and insist the rest of the club listen respectfully until the speaker wore down or, what was more likely, the time for the meeting expired.

By a literal luck of the draw (Brenda had pulled my name out of the hat), I got to play guinea pig, testing our latest approach to normalcy. So I spent the better part of a week boning up on my topic, preparing a sizable stack of note cards and practicing for hours in front of a mirror while forgoing my favorite television shows, *The Wonder Years* and *NYPD Blue*. But even after all the hours of preparation, I still had qualms about stepping forward and speaking to the members. It wasn't because I felt ill prepared or wasn't familiar with the material. Heaven knows I already knew more about fallen flag railroads than most people would learn in a lifetime. No, I was more concerned how members would react during and after my presentation. Would they talk to one another while I was speaking? Would they nod off? Would they just follow Ethan's lead—get up and walk out?

When the fateful hour arrived, I moved to the front of the group, took a deep breath, and cast off into the deep: "My topic is fallen flag railroads—rail lines that disappeared because of merger or bankruptcy. At their peak there were some one hundred forty major railroad companies; but by the 1970s only four of those classic rail lines had survived with their names intact: the Canadian National, the Canadian Pacific, the Kansas City Southern, and the Union Pacific. That's right, the railroads you've heard in songs—Arlo Guthrie's Illinois Central, Johnny Cash's Rock Island Line, John Denver's Atchison, Topeka, and the Santa Fe—and the railroads you've bought and mortgaged— the Pennsylvania, the B & O, and even the Reading on which you passed 'Go' and collected two hundred dollars. They're all gone now. Only memories…"

As I paused briefly to reflect on the past, Casper jumped up, walked in front of me bouncing his basketball, and then exited the gym. But hell-bent now on finishing my talk, I ignored the distraction and quickly picked up the thread. "You know, we've had a number of fallen flag railroads here in Tennessee, including the Louisville & Nashville, the Memphis and

Charleston, the NC&StL, and the Nashville and Northwestern, which during the early part of the Civil War only ran westward some twenty-five miles from Nashville to Kingston Springs. But after the Union army captured Nashville and made the city its headquarters for the western theater, the bluecoats decided to extend the railroad westward some fifty miles to the Tennessee River. This rail extension would allow the Feds to move supplies from the Ohio River valley down the Tennessee River to a port at Johnsonville where they would load the materials onto a Nashville and Northwestern express headed for the capital.

"Building this important extension from Kingston Springs to Johnsonville became a top priority and was finished in record time. So you might ask, 'Who were these fellows who accepted the challenge and completed the work so quickly?' Well, these men of the Thirteenth US Colored Infantry were heroes in every sense of the word. They not only helped build the railroad and then protect it from Confederate attacks, but they also played a crucial role in the Battle of Nashville in mid-December 1864.

"While the Thirteenth didn't see any real action the first day of the battle, they saw all they wanted the second afternoon. Colonel Hatensteine ordered his men to the foot of Overton's Hill on the rebels' right flank. At high noon a first wave of veteran troops charged up Overton's but were pushed back into the Thirteenth waiting in reserve at the bottom of the hill. The colonel then gave the order for the Thirteenth to make a charge. And as the men ran up the rise with their bayonets fixed, they heard bullets whistling past their heads and then making awful thudlike sounds as they ripped into their longtime friends.

"They tried holding the ground they'd taken on Overton's but were pushed back to the foot of the hill. A little later in the afternoon, they pulled themselves together, ran back up the rise, and finally took it. And as they sat tired and bloodied at the top of the hill, their commanding officer came by and praised them, saying the men of the Thirteenth had matched his finest soldiers in bravery 'and deeds of noble daring.'"

I then detailed several of the other fallen flag railroads of Tennessee: the Louisville & Nashville, the Memphis and Charleston, and the NC&StL, which used to run through Hollow Rock and Warfield on its way to Memphis. When I had finished reading the last note card, I looked up and asked almost pleadingly, "Are there any questions?" No one said anything. As usual, there would be no feedback, no reinforcement, no expression of interest in a topic I held dear to my heart. I gathered my note cards up from the table and shuffled back toward my chair, eyes on the ground. But as I neared my seat, a lone voice in the wilderness spoke up.

"The Short Line, Jason?"

I turned and gazed at Stats. I didn't say anything at first. I just smiled. I was too stunned to react immediately—not confounded by the question but by the fact that after all these years there had finally been a question—a query about something I really cared about. Stats had listened to me and was now engaging in honest dialogue. An unfamiliar shock of triumph surged through me. Those four simple words would remain with me the rest of my life.

Stats repeated his question. "Ah, the Short Line, Jason?"

I took a deep breath and asked for clarification. "The Short Line?"

"Yes, there are four railroads on the game board. You only mentioned three—the B&O, the Pennsylvania, and the Reading. So what happened to the Short Line? Did it merge or go bankrupt?"

I nodded and smiled. "It did neither. I didn't mention it because there never was a Short Line Railroad. As you know, Stats, the properties on the board are all associated with Atlantic City. Now there used to be a streetcar service there called the Shore Fast Line, and there was a railroad running through town called the Seashore Lines. So if I had to guess, I'd suspect Mr. Darrow, the game's inventor, got the idea for the Short Line Railroad from one of these two Atlantic City rail services."

"Hmm… so there never was a Short Line Railroad.… That's really interesting, Jason."

I puffed out my chest, pumped my fist into the air, and eased down into my chair.

Two weeks later it was Stats's time to step up to the plate. Since his older brother had made it to the majors and his father had played several seasons in the minor leagues, we suspected Stats would play his strong suit and dazzle us with

19

a barrage of arcane baseball facts and figures. We smiled as he cleared his throat and, true to form, began firing off one fact or statistic after another. "Contrary to popular belief Abner Doubleday didn't invent baseball in Elihu Phinney's cow pasture in Cooperstown, New York.

"Those honors go to Alexander Cartwright, whom Congress, in June 1953, officially declared the inventor of the modern pastime. Mr. Cartwright modeled baseball on the stick and ball game he'd played in a field near Fourth Avenue and Twenty-seventh Street in Manhattan. And the first known game with rules written by Mr. Cartwright was played across the Hudson River in Hoboken, New Jersey, in June 1845.

"Baseball is played on a diamond-shaped field anchored by a home plate, which is a five-sided wedge of rubber with a leading edge measuring seventeen inches, two adjacent sides measuring eight and a half inches, and a final two sides measuring twelve inches and set at forty-five-degree angles to form a point at the back of the plate. Three canvas bases fifteen inches square and set ninety feet apart round out the infield diamond. At the center of this ninety-by-ninety-foot square is the pitcher's mound. And at the center of this mound is another slab of rubber called the pitcher's plate, measuring six inches wide and two feet long. The leading edge of the pitcher's plate is exactly sixty feet six inches from the back point of the home plate."

Stats paused briefly, allowing us to absorb the tidal wave of figures before he resumed his numerical blitz. "A baseball game has 12,386,344 possible plays, and through this year approximately eleven thousand players have ever had a chance to make one of them in the big leagues. Of the twelve million possible plays, the ones which stand out revolve mostly around hitting and pitching. And out of those eleven thousand or so players, one hitter and one pitcher stand alone at the top—Babe Ruth and Cy Young." Stats surveyed the room and asked, "Do y'all think it was easy for them to make it to the top?"

My fellow club members looked at each other, shrugged, and remained silent.

"Well, let's see then. In his autobiography, *The Babe Ruth Story,* the Bambino sums up his childhood in only five paragraphs—a little less than three hundred words. In fact, you could boil those paragraphs down to just two sentences. The Sultan of Swat said, 'I hardly knew my parents' and 'I had a rotten start, and it took me a long time to get my bearings.'

"Since the Babe's mother and father were both very much alive and he lived with them in downtown Baltimore, how could he claim, 'I hardly knew my parents' and 'I had a rotten start'?"

The Outcasts shrugged again.

"Well, I suspect it had a lot to do with a Wilkens Avenue trolley ride the Babe and his father took out to the suburbs in June 1902 when the boy was only seven years old."

I now returned the favor Stats had earlier bestowed on me. I asked him, "Where were they headed, Stats?"

He smiled and replied, "To an enormous gray, five-story building. A dark fortress surrounded by thick walls with the only exit and entrance through a set of huge iron gates."

"A rich man's castle?" Checkers asked.

"Oh, no, the farthest thing from it. With suitcase in hand the seven-year-old Babe entered the St. Mary's Industrial School for Orphan, Delinquent, Incorrigible, and Wayward Boys."

"But he wasn't an orphan!" I interjected.

"For all intents and purposes he was, Casey J. Ya see, before climbing aboard the trolley that morning, he'd already said good-bye to his mother. And before walking alone through those iron gates at St. Mary's, he'd given his father a final hug and said so long."

"But why did his parents throw him away?" Zulu asked.

"No one really knows for sure. It wasn't like he had a lot of brothers and sisters running around and his parents couldn't afford to feed 'em. I mean, he did have seven brothers and sisters, but all but one sister died at an early age. The only real clue we have is something the Babe said after growing up. He said, 'I was a bad kid.' So maybe his parents just couldn't control him. Who knows?"

"Did he ever get to leave the place while growing up?" Spokes asked.

"Yes, but only to attend his mother's funeral. He was twelve years old then."

Bones looked anxious. "When did he finally get to leave there for good?" she asked.

"I'll get there in a minute," Stats said patiently. "Now the Babe was supposed to stay at the reformatory until he was twenty-one, learn a trade before leaving. Ya see, it was like the military. The boys would get up at six in the morning, do some math, English, religion, and the like, and the rest of the day was devoted to work. The boys would rotate from job to job learning about the different trades: carpentry, steam fitting, tailoring, baking, shoemaking, farming, woodworking, and the like. And besides all the instruction they also took turns cooking the meals, sewing their own clothes, and taking care of the extensive grounds within the walls."

"Sounds more like prison than the army," I said. "Work, work, work."

"Yes, there was a lot of that for sure," Stats responded. "But there was also some time for recreation. Most of the eight hundred or so boys played baseball on the grounds, assigned to various leagues based on talent. The Babe later estimated he played in over two hundred games a year while at St. Mary's—catching, playing third base, pitching. In fact, by the time he was eighteen, he was the best pitcher at the orphanage and was permitted on weekends to leave St. Mary's to play on local teams. The following year—someway, somehow—the Babe signed with the minor league Baltimore Orioles, and the rest is history. At the time of his retirement, his major league records included most home runs in a season, most home runs in a career, highest slugging percentage, most intentional walks, twelve home-run titles, thirteen slugging crowns, and six RBI titles.

"So a ninety-by-ninety-foot square of possibility within St. Mary's walls launched a forsaken kid on a magical ride across the country where he rubbed shoulders with kings and presidents; stood at the back of rail cars in the middle of the night and waved to crowds that had gathered just to catch a glimpse; stopped in farm and mill towns to greet fans who'd never have a chance to see him play and would then hit long drives off the best pitchers the communities had to offer; and perhaps most importantly, never forgetting his roots, the Babe dropped in on the boys at orphanages, offering them advice. 'Never let the fear of striking out get in your way,' he would say. 'It's hard to beat a person who never gives up.'

"His Boston Red Sox teammate, outfielder Harry Hooper, pretty much summed up the Babe's journey when he said, 'You know, I saw it all happen from beginning to end. But sometimes I still can't believe what I saw…. I saw a man transformed from a human being into something pretty close to a god. If somebody had predicted that on the Boston Red Sox back in 1914, he would have been thrown into an insane asylum.'"

At that point Mrs. Prescott entered the gym. "Excuse me, Kevin. We're just about out of time today."

"Out of time, Mrs. P.? Geez. I haven't even finished Ruth yet, and I still have Cy Young to go!"

"You'll have to save it for another day after everyone else has had a turn. You can pick up right where you left off. It'll give everyone something to look forward to."

"May I add one more thing, though, Mrs. P.?"

"Sure, Kevin, but keep it brief. The buses will be here soon."

"As a preview for my next talk then, I just want y'all to know the greatest pitcher ever, Cy Young, was traded from a minor league club to a major league team for a suit of clothes early on in his career! That's all I'll have to say for now, Mrs. P."

"Thanks, Kevin. So when the group meets again next time, I believe it'll be Sandra's turn to speak."

After this second successful meeting of our social club, it was time to return to the jungle and continue our struggle of fending off the beasts. For neurotypicals, the playground, the hallway, and the cafeteria were welcome social venues, respites from the classroom with its day-in-and-day-out drudgery of grammar, social studies, and math.

But for us Outcasts it was the opposite. The only places we ever really felt safe *were* the classroom and the gymnasium, where we held our club meetings. For us, the playground, the hallway, and the cafeteria were nothing more than free-fire zones where Tommy, Billy, and/or Johnny could wreak "accidental" havoc on Stats, Bones, Zulu, and me with little fear of reprisal or administrative punishment. Every time we Outcasts would leave a classroom, we held our collective breath, knowing we were entering a threatening space where, as this triumvirate of bullies liked to remind us, "shit just happened."

And today was no different than any other as I took a deep breath and stepped out into the usual minefield, cradling a tray loaded with my all-time favorite school lunch—two cartons of chocolate milk, a heaping bowl of ham and bean soup, and a huge helping of tuna fish sandwiched between two pieces of thick, toasted rye. After spotting the Outcast table at the farthest reaches of the room, I picked up the pace, walking with my head down to avoid eye contact. Eye contact, I had learned, could lead to a full spectrum of verbal abuse: everything from groaning and muttering to taunting and outright threats.

As I approached safe harbor thinking, "Whew! Dodged another bullet today," a musclebound chest—was it Tommy, Billy, or Johnny this time?—slammed into my side, sending my milk, soup, and sandwich crashing to the floor. Stunned and embarrassed, I immediately dropped to my knees and literally began trying to pick up the pieces—the pieces of ceramic bowl, which had shattered into a thousand shards on impact.

Within seconds a ring of faces stood over me chanting the usual taunts: "Dickhead!"... "Asshole!"... "Numbnuts!"... "Klutz!" The mocking continued it seemed for hours until Mrs. Jasper, the cafeteria supervisor, broke up the merry band, stepped in, and exclaimed, "Oh no, Jason. Not this again!" She turned to one of the perps and said, "Billy, go fetch Mr. Jacobs. Tell him to bring a mop and bucket to clean up a big spill." She then looked back down at me, shook her head, and muttered, "Jason, what in the world are we going to do with you?"

I didn't respond. I just looked down and shouted silently from my knees, "*With me*, Mrs. Jasper? What are you going to do *with me*?"

Stats was by my side then and together we gathered my ruined meal and carried it to the trash. With no time to get back in line, I got a Twinkie and a can of root beer out of the vending machine. Another lunch spoiled.

As we settled into our seats for Bones's presentation at the next club meeting, we understood we were in for a real challenge, first trying to understand the material and then staying focused on a very difficult topic. After all, she had earned her nickname because of her consuming interest in embryology and developmental anatomy. But to her credit, Bones tried making her material more accessible by borrowing an overhead projector from our science teacher, Mr. Miles, and creating a stack of transparencies to provide drawings of what she was describing in her talk.

Bones flipped on the switch and positioned the first transparency on the projector. It read: "An Introduction to Embryogeny." She surveyed the room and declared, "Every one of you sitting out there is made up of a hundred trillion cells." As she placed the second transparency on the projector, a drawing entitled "A Fertilized Egg," Bones said, "But every one of you started out as a single cell! Now did any of you ever stop to think how you got from here"—she pointed to the egg—"to there?" She rotated so that her finger now pointed to all of us Outcasts in the audience. No one moved a muscle.

"Well, once that single cell divides, becomes a hollow ball of cells, and attaches to the female, it's called a blastocyst. It looks something like what you see here on this third transparency. And then once this blastocyst attaches to the female, the magic—no, the *miracle*—really begins. Instructions buried deep within the embryonic cells cause them to separate into three basic cell types—ectoderm, mesoderm, and endoderm—and then move about on the surface of the blastocyst. As you can see here on the fourth transparency, the ectoderm eventually slows and stays put, but the endoderm and mesoderm continue moving toward an opening, the blastopore, and then dive down through the hole into the hollow at the center of the blastocyst, the lumpy ball there. So what's the importance of these three cell types?" Still no one moved.

Bones positioned a fifth transparency on the projector, this one entitled "From Embryo to Adult," and said, "The innermost layer of cells in the blastocyst, the endoderm, is programmed to become organs like your bladder, your liver, and your lungs. The second layer of cells within the inner space of the blastocyst, the mesoderm, is designed to produce structures like your heart, your skeletal muscles, and your blood vessels. And that layer of cells that stayed put on the outer surface of the blastocyst, the ectoderm, is programmed to become things like your skin, the lens of your eye, the spinal cord, and your brain.

"But how does all this cell differentiation and movement get set into motion? How does a clump of cells turn into various tissues, glands, and organs? And how does all of this finally become a living, breathing baby? Well, the answers lie in your genes, in your DNA. As you can see on this sixth transparency here, each of your cells contains forty-six chromosomes carrying somewhere between sixty thousand and one hundred thousand genes. And while all these cells contain the same numbers and types of genes, the cells don't all look alike, and they don't all do the same thing. Some are heart cells; others are lung cells, blood cells, or cells destined to become the lining of your stomach or your intestines.

"But if the cells contain the same numbers and types of genes, why then do the cells look different and perform different tasks? Well, it's because different groups of genes get switched on in the various cells. And when certain genes are turned on, they direct that cell to make a specific protein which defines its shape and function."

"But how does a cell know which particular genes to turn on to create the right protein?" I asked. "I read somewhere there are some sixty-four trillion potential gene combinations."

"That's right," Bones replied. "It's not entirely clear, but the experts think the genes take their cue from the location of the cell in the embryo. And the cells talk to one another through chemical messaging." Bones paused, surveyed her audience, which had hung in there with her admirably so far, and then continued reflectively, "But when you stop to think about the trillions of possible gene combinations and the billions of messages sent and received during development, you can see how mistakes can cause us to end up with cystic fibrosis, Down syndrome, sickle-cell anemia, autism, hyperactivity, obsessive-compulsive tendencies, and so on."

Stats jumped in. "What's the likelihood of being born with a birth defect then?"

Bones smiled sardonically and answered, "We Outcasts, we're in the three percent."

And then like clockwork, Mrs. Prescott appeared at the door and shouted, "Time to wrap it up!"

As I lay in bed that night reflecting on our first three presentations, I concluded an impartial observer might plausibly view our talks as polemics rather than stand-alone presentations depicting our obsessions with particular topics. I could see this reasonable observer establishing a comfortable glass-half-full versus glass-half-empty continuum where Stats plays the optimist and Bones the pessimist; where Stats sees the possibilities and Bones the limitations; and where Stats strives for the light while Bones curses the darkness oppressing the three percent.

Reasonable interpretation? Yes. Credible analysis? Certainly. Understandable finding? Absolutely. But sad to say, an inaccurate conclusion based on faulty assumptions about us Outcasts and that comfortable half-full/half-empty continuum.

The reasonable observer might assume that our Outcast ledgers remain static and absolute, where some of us three percenters are perpetual pessimists while others of us soldier on as eternal optimists. But nothing is ever as clear-cut as that. Truth is malleable. The continuum doesn't exist in a theoretical vacuum but in our souls, in our everyday lives. Mutability reigns every second, minute, and hour of every day in all of us, even in us Outcasts. And in an odd sort of way it's comforting to note that you neurotypicals and we Outcasts are all tossed about together in this same lifeboat. We all rise at daybreak, and the pendulum begins swinging in wide human arcs from hallelujah hope to devastating despair.

3

WHILE THE FIRST AND third Tuesday afternoons were devoted to the Poker Flats Social Club, the second and fourth were reserved for a well-intentioned retooling project on behalf of four of us McGill Outcasts. To her credit, our guidance counselor, Mrs. Prescott, had identified telltale traits that Bones, Stats, Zulu, and I shared. Besides our tendency to focus obsessively on specific subjects, we rarely made eye contact; had difficulty reading people's gestures and tone of voice; encroached on our classmates' personal space; interrupted others while trying to conduct one-sided conversations; engaged in occasional outbursts; and had an inability to see things from our classmates' perspectives.

Based on her observations, Mrs. Prescott concluded—and correctly, I should add—we four Outcasts found social interaction confusing and overwhelming; found it extremely difficult to predict or understand the intent or actions of others; and thus found it nearly impossible to form lasting friendships with neurotypicals. So with her heart and professionalism in the right place, Mrs. Prescott sought help from Dr. Green, the junior high psychologist, who arranged for Ms. Tabor, a special ed teacher, to conduct communication and interpersonal skills training while the good doctor provided us the more advanced group behavioral therapy.

Realizing the four of us Outcasts learned the unwritten rules of spontaneous communication in a rote fashion much as a student learns a foreign language, Ms. Tabor and Dr. Green adopted a step-by-step approach to improving our interpersonal skills and managing our "problematic behaviors." Once we had memorized the four or five steps (or rules) to a new skill, we engaged in role-play to reinforce the desired behavior.

On the first day of our social skills workshop, Ms. Tabor strolled into the room, wrote the word *Listening* on the whiteboard, and said, "The ability to listen to others is the foundation—the key—to establishing lasting friendships. Mrs. Prescott tells me she's been working with y'all informally through your social club on improving your listening skills. What I want to do here beginning today is give you a step-by-step set of rules to help you further improve those skills." She turned to the board and wrote, "1. Look directly at the person who is speaking." She turned, moved toward us, and elaborated, "The first step in effective listening is to face the speaker. Establish eye contact briefly from time to time. And remember, don't stare!"

Ms. Tabor returned to the whiteboard and wrote, "2. Concentrate on what the speaker is saying." She turned to us again and emphasized, "You let the person know you're listening by nodding occasionally and interjecting two or three 'uh-huhs' along the way." She walked back to the board and wrote the next step. "3. Wait! Don't interrupt! Don't talk out of turn!" Ms. Tabor turned around and warned, "Don't show any signs of impatience, like looking around at everything else, fidgeting, or starting to ease away from the conversation." She then wrote the next step: "4. When it's your turn, express yourself clearly." She turned around and explained, "Say what you feel. Say what you think. And ask questions to advance the conversation. This is what we call 'active listening.'" She scanned our small semicircle of Outcasts and asked, "Any questions so far?"

We all shook our heads while staring at the floor.

"Okay, then… but before we can become good listeners, someone has to start a conversation. So what are the steps to getting started?" Ms. Tabor returned to the whiteboard and wrote, "1. Greet the other person." She turned, walked toward us, and explained, "Look the person in the eye, say 'hello,' and shake their hand." She returned to the board and wrote, "2. Chitchat. Make small talk for a while." "For example," she said, turning, "talk about the weather, school sports, a new movie coming out." She then wrote the next step on the board: "3. Determine if the other person is engaged in the conversation." "Ask yourself, 'Is the other person looking at me?' 'Are they nodding?' 'Are they interjecting an "uh-huh" now and then?' These are your clues." She returned to the board and wrote, "4. Introduce your main topic." Turning again, she moved toward our semicircle and encouraged us, "Make your pitch! Say what you really are there to talk about." She paused briefly and asked, "Any questions?"

Again, the four of us shook our heads while staring at the floor.

"Well, okay, then. Let's practice our conversation and listening skills. I need two volunteers to come up and sit in the chairs here. Who's going to be our brave guinea pigs today?"

Stats and I glanced over at each other and thrust our hands into the air.

Ms. Tabor smiled and motioned for us to step forward and take a seat. As we settled into the chairs facing each other, Ms. Tabor asked, "So, in our first role-play here, which of you boys wants to be the speaker?" Stats got his hand up a millisecond before I did. Ms. Tabor declared him the winner and announced, "Okay, then, Kevin, you'll start the conversation and put our friend Jason here to the test. Stand up now. All set?"

We nodded and mumbled simultaneously, "All set."

As Ms. Tabor stepped to the side, she made a loud clicking noise with her tongue while shutting an imaginary clapperboard. She then shouted lightheartedly, "Lights! Camera! Action!"

Stats jumped right into the scene. He extended his hand and said, "Hi, Casey J., good to see ya!"

I extended my hand and responded, "Ditto, Stats."

"What ya been up to?"

"Nothing much. Keeping my nose in the math books."

"Yeah, me too. It's been a bear." Stats paused briefly and then moved onto familiar turf. "Ya happen to see the seventh and deciding game of the 2001 World Series last night? They reran it on the Classic Sports Network."

"Nope. Had to go with my mom and dad into McGill. Mama had a concert on the Pantheon campus. Dad's got me helping out with the sound system when she plays locally. So what about the game?"

"One of the greatest ever. Two twenty-game winners facing off. Schill pitching for the Diamondbacks and the Rocket for the Yankees. Dueled to a 1–1 tie through seven innings."

"Schill? The Rocket?"

"Yeah. Curt Schilling and Roger Clemens. Two of the best hurlers ever. Well, anyway, after Soriano hit a solo homer off of Schill in the eighth giving the Yankees the lead, the Diamondbacks brought in the Big Unit in relief."

"The Big Unit?"

"Yeah. Randy Johnson. Well, anyway, the Diamondbacks were really rolling the dice with that move."

"How so?"

"The Big Unit had started the previous night. Pitched seven innings. Threw a hundred and four pitches! And here he was now back on the field with all the marbles on the table. And with the chips down, he closed the Yankees out in the eighth and then again in the ninth, leaving it up to the Diamondback hitters to overcome a 2–1 deficit in the bottom of the ninth. A tall order, too. They were facing the Sandman."

"The Sandman?"

"Yeah. Mariano Rivera. One of the greatest relievers ever. Well, anyway, with one out and two on, Womack lined a double down the right-field line, scoring the runner from second base and tying the game."

"Wow!"

"Yeah, getting tense. Well, anyway, still with only one out, the Diamondbacks loaded the bases, bringing up Gonzo."

"Gonzo?"

"Luis Gonzalez, the Diamondbacks' best hitter and MVP. So with one out, bases loaded, the Yankee infield pulled in to cut off the run at the plate. Oh and one count on Gonzo." Stats paused, shook his head, and said, "And this is where it got spooky."

"Spooky?"

"Yeah. McCarver, the color man on the broadcast, suggested the Sandman might have trouble with Gonzo."

"How's that?"

"McCarver said, 'The one problem the Yankees have is Rivera throws inside to left-handed hitters, and the batters get a lot of broken-bat singles to the shallow outfield. And that's the danger of bringing the infield in with a guy like Rivera on the mound.'"

"Okay… but spooky?"

"Yeah, because that's exactly what happened. One out, bases loaded, the Yankee infield pulled in to cut off the run at the plate. The count is 0 and 1. Gonzo swings hard, just gets a piece of the ball, pops it up over Jeter's head at shortstop, just out of his reach and barely making it to the outfield, but it's enough to score the winning run from third! And the crowd went wild!"

"Geez, Stats! Don't tell my parents, but I'm sorry I missed it."

"Me too, Casey J. Me too."

As we turned and faced our grand audience of two, Ms. Tabor shouted, "Bravo! Bravo! Let's here it for Kevin and Jason."

And when Zulu and Bones began applauding, Stats and I took several exaggerated bows, admittedly showing off in front of the girls.

"Okay, fellows, take your seats, and let's discuss how you thespians performed." Ms. Tabor turned to Brenda and asked, "Did Kevin start the conversation with a greeting?"

"Yes, ma'am," Brenda replied. "Kevin said, 'Hi,' and shook Jason's hand."

"Okay. Now, Sandra, look at the second step on the board there under 'Starting a Conversation.' Did Kevin make small talk with Jason?"

"Yes, ma'am," Sandra answered. "Kevin asked Jason what he'd been up to."

"Very good, Sandra. And, Brenda, was there any way for Kevin to know Jason was listening?"

"Yes, ma'am. Jason was breaking into the conversation asking questions about what Kevin was saying."

"That's right. So do the two of you think Jason was a good listener then?"

Bones and Zulu answered simultaneously, "Yes, Ms. Tabor."

"Did Jason face Kevin and make eye contact?"

They nodded, "Uh-huh."

"Did Jason fidget or try to back out of the conversation?"

"No, ma'am."

"Now we've already said Jason asked questions. So does this mean they both did a good job—Kevin starting the conversation and Jason listening effectively?"

Bones and Zulu nodded again. "Yes, Ms. Tabor."

"So y'all have any questions about starting a conversation or active listening? Anyone?" She looked at us a moment but no one spoke. "Well, okay then. But before we call it quits for the day, I want to remind you that the steps we've listed for these first two skill sets are rules we memorize and consider before acting in public. While we've openly discussed the steps here, we keep them to ourselves in our everyday lives. If we commit these rules to memory and practice them repeatedly, they'll help us appear more spontaneous and natural."

Two weeks later we Outcasts were back in the same room sitting in the same semicircle waiting for Dr. Green to appear and launch her behavioral therapy workshop. The authorization letter that went home to our parents said we would not only be learning techniques to help with our obsessions and meltdowns, but we would be developing skills to recognize pressure situations, understand our feelings while undergoing them, and then choose effective strategies to cope with potential anxiety, anger, and unhappiness.

Dr. Green entered the room some fifteen minutes late; and without offering an explanation or apology, she moved straight to the whiteboard and wrote in large block letters, "UNDERSTANDING OUR EMOTIONS." She then turned and said, "Our minds and bodies are closely connected. When we respond emotionally to someone's words or actions, our bodies tend to react physically. And if we tune in to our physical reactions, we can use them to help us understand precisely what we are feeling. So what then are the steps we need to take to understand our emotions?"

She turned back to the board and wrote, "Step 1. Become aware of your physical reactions/sensations." She walked toward our semicircle and said, "For example, we might feel a tightness in our chests. We might turn red. We might feel queasy." Dr. Green returned to the board and wrote, "Step 2. Understand why you feel the way you do." She explained, "You have to ask yourself, 'What did they say or do that caused me to have this physical reaction? Did they tease me? Threaten me? Compliment me?'" Dr. Green then wrote the next step on the board: "Step 3. Determine how you would classify the feeling." She turned and said, "Did you feel joy? Embarrassment? Fear? You see, we have to identify the feeling before we can take the next important step."

Dr. Green paused, moved back to the board, and wrote in large block letters, "REACT." She turned toward us, repeated the three rules of the previous skill set, and explained, "Once we know what we're feeling, we are then prepared to take the next two steps." She returned to the whiteboard and wrote, "Step 1. Ask yourself, 'How should I react?'" She turned to us and said, "So you ask yourself, Would it be better to say nothing and walk away? Delay a discussion until you've had a chance to consider the right place and time for a conversation? Or determine the best way to express your emotion—for example, with a tinge of humor or respectful directness and then…" She paused, returned to the board and wrote, "Step 2. Retreat, Delay, or Express what you're feeling." Turning back to face us, she said, "And if you decide to express your feelings, then say what you mean and mean what you say. You might not always get it just right. But these steps will help you avoid many of the pitfalls leading to misunderstandings, embarrassment, and, even worse, angry confrontations."

Dr. Green slowed the express just long enough to consult her watch, catch her breath, and construct a segue to a third skill set. She returned to the board and wrote in all caps, "EMPATHY." She then moved back toward our semicircle and said, "In building relationships it's not only important to understand our own emotions but to make every attempt to appreciate the feelings of others. So what are the rules to creating effective empathy?" On the whiteboard she wrote, "Step 1. Observe the other party." She turned and advised us, "Ask yourself, 'What are the person's facial expressions? What is their tone of voice? What is their body language?'" And then it was back to the whiteboard to write, "Step 2. Listen carefully to what the other party is saying." She turned and said, "Focus on the context *and* the content of what they're saying." Next Dr. Green wrote, "Step 3. Identify the feelings associated with what the person is saying." "Ask yourself," she said, "do they appear angry? Worried? Sad?" Returning to the whiteboard she wrote, "Step 4. Decide the best way to let the person know you understand what they are saying." Here she paused a moment. "You could nod as they speak," she suggested. "You could pat them on the arm. You could tell them you are sorry they are going through such rough times." With a brief nod of the head, she turned and wrote the final rule on the board, "Step 5. Act!" As she turned back around, Dr. Green glanced at her watch again, scanned our semicircle, and asked her first and only question of the day, "Is all of this beginning to make sense?"

At first we four Outcasts sat there in stunned silence, staring at the floor embarrassed. But something within us compelled us to at least acknowledge the effort by nodding, even if we had serious doubts about the stepwise approach, the content, and her total-immersion, blitzkrieg style of delivery.

Dr. Green smiled and responded, "Very good then. So if there are no questions, I'll see y'all again in two weeks when we'll discuss 'Overcoming Failures,' 'Reacting to Teasing,' and 'Coping with Being Excluded.'" She then quickly gathered up her notebooks and disappeared stage right as if rushing off to another meeting.

That night I ran into Stats at the pizza joint down the street, and after ordering a large thin crust with sausage and cheese, we found a table in the corner and shared our first impressions about Ms. Tabor and Dr. Green's retooling project. I took a sip of my root beer and asked, "What did you think of the first two classes?"

Stats smiled and replied, "If the rest of 'em are on par with the first two, I'd say they're above the Mendoza line... but nothing to write home about. Sure not Hall of Fame material, I guarantee you that."

"The Mendoza line?"

"Yeah, a mediocre .200 batting average, named for Mario Mendoza, a journeyman infielder. Played some eight years in the majors with the Pirates, the Mariners, and the Rangers. His Seattle teammates coined the phrase after realizing Mendoza hovered around .200 the entire season in four of five years—from '75 through '79."

"So then, what's the cutoff for the Hall?"

"Oh, right around a .250 batting average for position players. Anyone under .250 who made the Hall is either a pitcher or a manager."

"So you'd rate our classes somewhere between .200 and .250, huh?"

"Yeah, sounds about right to me. What about you, Casey J.?"

"About right for me, too. The classes are so much like painting by numbers. It's not like the free flow of a masterpiece."

"Uh-huh. I'd describe it like… like they're breaking down a golf swing. 'Ya see, boys and girls, ya first address the ball, making sure of your balance and the width of your stance. Next ya start your backswing, making sure ya bring your club up and in while rotating your hips away from the green. Then as ya start your downswing, ya make sure your club stays on the same plane as your backswing and your weight transfers to your lead leg. Then at the point of impact, ya make sure your body's aligned with the flag so your club face strikes the ball squarely. Then, boys and girls, on your follow-through ya make sure the club shaft goes up and in as your shoulders and hips rotate around toward the flag. And then finally, students, you watch your ball invariably sail off into the water or into the woods.'"

I laughed at the truth in his lame joke and then responded seriously. "I think we're on the same page, Stats. The classes are just too mechanical. A lot to remember when you're walking up to someone to say hello. Nothing like the artist who spontaneously sees the painting in her head. She's not running her finger down the page trying to discover that twenty-two is magenta and forty-three is burnt umber. She just paints the image she sees in her mind."

"Yeah, and it's the same for the professional golfer. He frames the shot. Sets up after a practice swing. And then arcs the ball up over the hazards onto the green five feet from the flag. Sure not like us amateurs going through our checklists: How's my balance? How's the width of my stance? Is my club moving away from the ball on the right plane? And on and on and on. And what do I get for all my trouble? My club digs into the ground a full two inches behind the ball, launching an embarrassing moon shot and a divot the size of a quarter-acre lot. And to top it all off, I get another lecture from my father about my downswing and follow-through."

"So tell me, Stats, with all that going on, how'd you manage to get the workshops up to between .200 and .250?"

"Ah, I suspect Ms. Tabor's rules about listening and starting a conversation will come in handy with adults—ya know, teachers, parents, aunts, uncles, and the like—but probably not so much with our classmates, the 'normal' ones. They almost

43

immediately sense we're different when they meet us for the first time."

I chimed in. "Yeah, takes 'em little more than five minutes, and they know."

The waitress glided over to our table. "Excuse me, boys, large thin crust with sausage and cheese. Can I get ya anything else?"

"Two more root beers, please."

"Comin' right up."

"Thank ya, ma'am."

After savoring several generous slices of west Tennessee's finest thin crust with sausage and cheese, I eased us back into the conversation. "Okay, Stats, so keep on going now. Tell me, how did you manage to get the classes up to something between .200 and .250?"

"Well, I divided each of the workshops into two parts—the past and the future. We've experienced the first two workshops now, and we've seen the outlines of what's to come. So we can give a score to each of the classes we've attended so far. And then we can project a score for the future classes based on the material to be covered and its potential usefulness."

"So if I'm gripping with you so far, you've got four numbers—a past and future score for each of the two teachers. Right?"

"Yep. So I gave Ms. Tabor *almost* full credit for her first class… and a zero for the remaining weeks. The future classes look like a dry hole—'Saying I'm Sorry,' 'Becoming a Part of the Crowd,' 'Making Introductions.' Doesn't look like they'll be advancing the ball too far down the field."

"So what about Dr. Green? How did ya score her past and future classes?"

"Goose eggs all around! So when I add it all up for Ms. Tabor and Dr. Green, I get to a batting average somewhere between .200 and .250."

"But goose eggs for Dr. Green?"

"No doubt in my mind, Casey J. A shutout the whole way. She starts the course off telling us to get in touch with our bodies, to become aware of our physical reactions. Telling us to sense the lumps in our throats, the knots in our stomachs. Telling us to discover what our classmates are doing to make us feel the way we do. My God, Dr. Green, that's too easy! They're taunting us! Threatening us! Bullying us! And then she goes on telling us to classify the sensations as either joy, embarrassment, or fear—as if we've never experienced anything remotely close to the terror, insomnia, and vomiting that follow after confronting thugs twice our size. And your list of feelings, Dr. Green? We think you've missed a few. What about our anger, our loneliness, our disappointments. Our fear of being isolated. Of being alone forever."I just nodded. I didn't want to get in front of this four-engine freight rumbling past the crossing gates.

"So what's next, Dr. Green? You say 'react'? And what are our choices, Dr. Green? You say we have three? And they are? Oh, so we can walk away. Or we can delay a response until later. Or we can speak up right then and there. But what happens if we walk away, Dr. Green?"

I jumped in and responded, "The taunting, threatening, and bullying just gets worse. It encourages them to ratchet up the torture."

"Ya hear that, Dr. Green? Walking away just makes things worse. So what about this delaying a response until we've had a chance to think through what we want to say? Waiting until the circumstances and the timing are right? But what happens if we delay our response, Dr. Green?"

"We never get around to speaking up," I said. "We live with our silence."

"Ya hear that, Dr. Green? Delaying is just like walking away, and it just makes things worse. So what about expressing ourselves right then and there? What happens then, Dr. Green?"

"We vent our frustrations and then suffer detentions or suspensions for what the counselors, teachers, and principals diagnose as our 'uncalled-for' meltdowns."

"Ya hear that, Dr. Green? Detentions and suspensions for striking back!" Stats paused to catch his breath. When he was calmer he said, "So now that we're in touch with our own feelings, Dr. Green, what do you suggest we do next?"

I offered up, "Empathize!"

"Empathize? Appreciate the feelings of others? And how do you propose we do that? What's the rule, Dr. Green?"

"Watch the other person," I said. "Observe their facial expressions. Are they angry? Worried? Sad?"

"I'm sorry, Dr. Green, but that's not our forte. We observe facial expressions using a part of the brain you use to look at lampshades or doors. And you want us to interpret the subtleties? The nuances in your smiles? Your frowns? The arching of your brows? My God, Dr. Green, we can't even tell if you're crying or not! So what's the backup plan then, Dr. Green?"

"Listen carefully to what the other person is saying. Focus on the context *and* the content of what they're saying."

"Hold on there a minute, Dr. Green. Ya want us to listen and focus on context and content, when we tend to interpret things literally? There must be a joke in there somewhere, but we are not getting it! So what then, Dr. Green?"

"Decide how you want to let the person know you feel their pain."

"And how do ya propose we do that, Dr. Green, when we barely understand what they're feeling at that point? So what do we do? Fake it? Stroke their arm? Nod and say we're sorry they're going through such tough times?" Stats gazed into my eyes and asked, "Ya see now why I gave her last class a zero?"

I nodded. "No argument from me, Stats."

"And the future's not too bright either. Classes on dealing with failure, teasing, and being excluded? Now those will be uplifting for sure!"

"I dunno, Stats, seems like we ought to give Dr. Green partial credit for at least trying to help."

"But giving points for confusing activity with accomplishment? Not where I come from. My father always says he buys results! And neither of these ladies has a snowball's chance of making it much above the Mendoza line and into the Hall of Fame. Why? Because they live in a different world from you and me, Casey J. They live in a parallel universe." He paused, stared at the wall for a few seconds, and then said, "Ya know, now that I think about it… maybe we should flip this whole thing on its ear. Why should we be the ones treated as outcasts for everyone else's lack of knowledge, kindness, and understanding?""Yeah, Stats. How about we get everyone else in a room—our teachers, classmates, counselors, parents. And then you, Bones, Zulu, and I teach them all a workshop in what it means living in our world. Living from the inside out. Explaining how it feels when they're constantly misinterpreting our words and actions, jumping to conclusions, and thinking the worst of us when we only had the best intentions in mind. Yeah, I can see it now. Classes defining the problems—'Judging,' 'Criticizing,' 'Shunning'—and other classes offering solutions—'Empathy,' 'Acceptance,' 'Inclusion'—leading to the desired outcome, 'Harmony.'"

4

A S HIGH SCHOOL JUNIORS and seniors, Bones, Stats, Zulu, and I occasionally crossed the social Rubicon from exiled freaks to tolerable nerds. But I don't want to leave a wrong impression here. It's not as if overnight we had become Mr. and Miss Congeniality, homecoming king and queen, or class president and secretary. Rather, we knowingly and willingly entered into a symbiotic compact with our classmates. In exchange for our acknowledged expertise in word-processing, spreadsheet, and presentation applications, we gained entrée into their world for a few fleeting minutes before being relegated again to what Stats affectionately referred to as "the cyber bullpen."

Now you might question our eagerness to prostitute ourselves for such a short-term high. But as my dad likes to say, you have to walk in someone else's shoes before you can fairly pass judgment on their behavior. And for the four of us it had been a long, winding, rocky road up through our sophomore year. We had wandered aimlessly in the wilderness shunned by our peers and intellectually victimized by many well-intentioned but poorly trained overseers who wrongly mistook our lack of social interaction, teamwork, and collaboration for laziness, obstinacy, and disobedience. Few understood that while we desperately wanted to belong to their world, we just weren't sufficiently wired to navigate their social rapids. Group projects for us were always intellectual exercises about the quest for truth and solving problems rather than getting along with teammates and worrying endlessly about peer feelings and perceptions.

So is it any wonder, then, that we Outcasts of Poker Flats would be drawn to all things computer? We had learned early on we didn't have to converse with our machines, entertain them, or tolerate any confusing mood swings. They never stepped backward when we approached, turned their backs when we tried to enter a conversation, rolled their eyes and groaned when we raised our hands in class, or muttered "Here we go again" when we got to rolling on one of our favorite topics. No, they were a rational, consistent, and predictable refuge from the maelstrom of our everyday lives. In a way our machines were like us. They could process hard, cold data. They just couldn't handle the emotional stuff very well.

In contrast to our elementary school classmates, we had drawn few strong hands along the way. But one of the few we had been dealt was the early introduction of computers into our homes thanks to the special ed teacher's recommendation. She had convinced our parents that personal computers running much of the same software we used at school would help level the playing field "to some degree."

And what began in elementary school as supervised individual exercises completed at home in the evenings inexorably morphed into unsupervised group competitions by the time we Outcasts reached junior high. Since the four of us lived within walking distance of one another, we would arrange to meet after school most days and spend hours playing games in rooms bedecked with computer posters and elegant network schematics. Some of us with an artistic bent even crafted a few uproarious tech placards including "When You Step In It: Reboot," "127.0.0.1 Is Where My Heart Is," and "Let Me Disambiguate That For You: NO!"

When we reflect on the few truly seismic events shaping our lives, we invariably recollect them and their seemingly trivial antecedents with remarkable clarity and precision. Even years before encountering a life-altering experience our psyches compel us to store random, ostensibly unrelated events for recall at a later date. And so it is we four Outcasts remember precisely every detail of what happened before, during, and after we were handed the keys to the kingdom.

Since we were nearing the Christmas break, I suspect our fifth-grade taskmaster, Mrs. Summerfield, wanted to surprise us with something special, a gift of sorts, which would entertain us, in keeping with the upcoming holidays, while simultaneously educating us, in keeping with her highest calling in life. At the end of school the day before, Mrs. Summerfield had distributed a homework assignment instructing us to review the words and place names listed on the pages; refer to the chapter "Expansion and Manifest Destiny" in our history textbooks; and write several sentences defining the words and describing each of the listed sites.

When we reached the history module the following afternoon, Mrs. Summerfield unexpectedly announced there would be a change in venue: "Okay, boys and girls, gather up your homework assignments, your texts, and your notebooks and follow me down the hallway *quietly* to the computer lab."

I looked over at Stats and said, "We must be living right. What did we do to deserve this?"

Stats smiled and shrugged. "I dunno. I guess they figure they owe us one. But whatever the reason, I'm sure glad we'll be getting out of here and finishing off the day in the lab."

A classmate, overhearing our exchange, butted in. "I don't know what y'all are so happy about. It's not like we got out of doing the homework or something."

Responding to his derisive tone I fired back a half-truth. "It's hard to explain, Bradley. We like the scenery in the lab and—"

Stats tapped my arm, pulling back on the reins. I stopped midsentence and repeated, "We like the scenery. Let's just leave it at that."

Enjoying the view in the lab was the truth in the half-truth. It was the only time during the day we ever saw sunlight. Unlike our windowless classroom, the lab's two six-by-twenty-four-inch slits in the outer wall allowed us to track the hours and the seasons. And if Stats hadn't put the brakes on, I would have revealed the unspoken other half of the whole truth via a biting rejoinder: "You see, Bradley, when our class steps into the lab, everything's turned upside down. Y'all are playing on our turf. Y'all struggle. We shine. Remember that first program we learned there years ago? KidsTime. Remember? It didn't take us long to put some distance between y'all and us 'losers,' as you like to say. Remember, Bradley? While y'all were still mastering Match-it and Dot-to-Dot, we Outcasts had moved on to writing songs on KidsNotes and tales on Story Writer. Remember *Number Munchers*, Bradley? It was Pac-Man meets the abacus. And while the Troggles were eating y'all alive in Multiples, we Outcasts were hanging out in Factors and Primes. Over and over the bad news flashed across your screens: 'Rats! You've been eaten by a Troggle.' And as y'all pounded your fists on the desks, we Outcasts smiled inside and played on, adding to our already sizable lead."

And the surprises kept coming that remarkable day. When we reached the lab, we discovered Mrs. Summerfield had managed to rig one of the computers to an overhead projector. The pull-down screen announced the subject of our homework, *The Oregon Trail: Expansion and Manifest Destiny*. Mrs. Summerfield moved to the front of the room beside the projector and began her lecture.

"Westward expansion started as a trickle," she said. "First there were the trappers, the fur traders, and explorers. Next the missionaries. And then the first emigrants. Following the call of destiny, a group of eighteen men set out from Peoria, Illinois, in May 1839 to colonize the Oregon country. These men of the 'Peoria Party' carried a flag announcing their goal, 'Oregon or the Grave.' And when all was said and done, ironically, half of them reached the Willamette Valley and the other half, makeshift cemeteries along the way."

Mrs. Summerfield paused and looked around the room. "Okay, class, now it's your turn to pick up the story. Jason, what happened four years later?"

"Ah… the Great Migration of '43."

"That's right. And, Kevin, how many people were a part of this Great Migration?"

"Somewhere between seven hundred and a thousand."

"Very good. And Bradley, who was their leader?

"Ah, John… John Gantt."

"Yes. And, Sandra, why do you suppose they chose him as leader and agreed to pay him one dollar per person?"

"Because he had been an officer in the army and a fur trader who knew the route."

"That's right. And by the way, Sandra, how far did Gantt agree to lead the party?"

"Ah, as far as Idaho. Fort Hall, Idaho."

"Very good. Let's stop here for a minute and review the primary route the Oregon Trail followed westward. Thomas, where did the trail begin?"

"Independence, Missouri."

"Yes, Thomas. And what other important trail started there?"

"The Santa Fe, Mrs. Summerfield."

"That's right. And, Billy, where'd the Oregon Trail go from Independence?"

"Across the Kansas River into Kansas."

"Yes, and, Gloria, after the trail crossed Kansas, where'd it go?"

"Over the Big Blue River into Nebraska."

"And, Warren, after Nebraska, what were the next two states?

"Ah… Wyoming and, ah, Idaho."

"Excellent. And after Idaho, Brenda?"

"Oregon, Mrs. Summerfield."

"Yes, that's right. And can you tell us where their final destination was in Oregon?"

"The Willamette Valley."

"Very good, Brenda. So the trail runs some two thousand miles westward from Independence, Missouri, to the Willamette Valley, Oregon. Now this next question wasn't part of your homework assignment, but does anyone know any of the cities located in the Willamette Valley? Anyone?" She waited for a volunteer but no one moved. "How about a hint. They're the largest cities in Oregon…. Still no takers? Okay, then. Running north to south, you have Portland, Salem, and Eugene. So you can see then the importance of the trail to the colonization of the Oregon country."

Mrs. Summerfield paused again briefly to regain her bearings. Then she said, "We noted that John Gantt had agreed to lead the Great Migration westward from Independence, Missouri, to Fort Hall, Idaho. But they still had a way to go to their final destination. So, Ethan, who agreed to lead the Great Migration from Fort Hall to the Willamette Valley?"

"Marcus Whitman."

"And this Marcus Whitman was one tough customer, wasn't he?"

We all nodded and mumbled in unison, "Uh-huh."

"That's right. And he was the right man for the job too, wasn't he?"

The class nodded again and said, "Yes, Mrs. Summerfield."

"That's right. Because this fellow had traveled east the year before from Oregon to St. Louis in the dead of winter and had survived the ordeal! So what better person to guide them? But before the party could leave Fort Hall, an argument broke out between Whitman and some experienced agents of the Hudson Bay Trading Company. What was their disagreement about, Jane?"

"Because of the condition of the trail the agents advised the settlers to abandon their wagons there at Fort Hall and use pack animals the rest of the way. But Mr. Whitman disagreed. He believed the party could take their wagons all the way to Oregon."

"Excellent. So what did the settlers decide to do, Jeffrey?"

"They took Whitman's advice and left Fort Hall in their wagons."

"That's right. Ya see, Whitman thought there were enough able-bodied men in the Migration to improve any roads that needed to be widened or blaze a trail through any forests standing in the way. So there was good news and bad news. The good news—Whitman was right about widening the roads and blazing trails through the rugged Blue Mountains of northeastern Oregon where the peaks ranged up to nine thousand feet. The bad news—when they reached the frontier town the Dalles, they were stopped in their tracks. So what stopped them, Jason?"

"There were no suitable roads for the wagons around Mount Hood."

"That's right, Jason. So did the settlers abandon their wagons there at the Dalles, thus proving Whitman wrong?"

"No, ma'am."

"What did Whitman suggest they do, Kevin?"

"Take the wagons apart and float them down the dangerous Columbia River."

"But what about the oxen and the other animals, Jane?"

"Some of the settlers led the animals around Mount Hood on the narrow, rugged Lolo Trail and eventually met up with the people who floated the wagons down the river."

"Excellent. And nearly all the folks in the Great Migration reached the Willamette Valley before winter set in, thus proving Whitman right! But more importantly, the Great Migration of '43 established a passable wagon trail from Independence, Missouri, to the Dalles, Oregon. And three years later the Barlow Road was finished, bypassing Mount Hood and thus creating a tough but acceptable passage from Independence, Missouri, to the Willamette Valley, Oregon."

Mrs. Summerfield smiled broadly as she moved over to the computer. She scanned the room and announced melodramatically, "Let's take a little expedition together out west and have some fun along the way, facing perils at every turn, fording treacherous rivers, contracting serious diseases, and hunting bison, bear, and deer to survive the difficult trip. What do you say? You ready to pull up stakes?"

We all responded in unison, "Yes, Mrs. Summerfield. Yes!" The teacher had achieved her goal: we were brimming with excitement.

"Well, westward ho, then! And we'll have all afternoon to complete our journey. I've reserved the computer lab for the rest of the school day." Mrs. Summerfield hit the space bar and read the opening menu projected on the screen. "You may (1) Travel the Trail, (2) Learn about the Trail, (3) See the Trail Top Ten, or (4) Turn the sound off."

She looked up from the projector and suggested, "Since we've already spent a great deal of time studying the Oregon Trail, how about we dive right into the game?"

Everyone eagerly shouted their agreement. "Travel the Trail! Travel the Trail!"

"I thought so," she said, laughing. "Okay, then, let's Travel the Trail."

A second menu appeared, and Mrs. Summerfield began reading aloud. "As Wagon Leader, what would you like to be? (1) A banker from Boston, (2) A carpenter, or (3) A farmer." She paused and then offered us some advice. "Let me give y'all a little hint. You get more money to spend on supplies as the banker. Any objections to being a banker from Boston?"

We all nodded enthusiastically.

As she made her selection, Mrs. Summerfield said, "Okay, then. A Boston banker it is!"

The next menu appeared, and she continued reading. "What is the Wagon Leader's first name? Ah, since we're playing this first game as a team and I'm running the computer, how about I be the Wagon Leader just this once? Everyone okay with that?"

We all nodded our approval.

She input "Betty" and hit the space bar; the next menu appeared. "What are the first names of the other four members of the party?"

A spontaneous confusion of fifth-grade humor especially from the Outcast contingent filled the air: "Larry!" "Tinker!" "Groucho!" "Moe!" "Evers!" "Harpo!" "Curly Joe!"

Mrs. Summerfield waved her hands and shouted lightheartedly, "Shh. Pipe down! Since everyone wants to be a comedian, I'll just have to call on someone and go with their suggestions." She closed her eyes and moved her hand back and forth across the room. The finger slowed and stopped. It was pointing at me. Mrs. Summerfield opened her eyes and said, "Well, it looks like Jason gets to do the honors today. Okay, Jason, so what are the first names of the other four members of our traveling party?"

A thought immediately came to mind. I wanted to share a little joke with my Outcast brother and sisters without raising the hackles of our classmates. I called out the names as if I were pulling them randomly from a telephone directory, "Uh, let's see. Duchess… Uncle Billy… um, Piney Woods… and, ah, Oakhurst."

"Very creative, Jason, an interesting, eclectic set of names you've conjured up there," Mrs. Summerfield said.

I glanced over at Stats, Zulu, and Bones, who had buried their faces in their hands fighting hard to hold back laughter. Victory, she is mine! Carl's Outcasts were sharing a strong invisible bond with one another and their thorny pasts.

After recording the manifest, Mrs. Summerfield read the next menu. "What month do you want to leave Independence?

(1) March, (2) April, (3) May, (4) June, (5) July, (6) Ask for advice." She paused briefly and then said, "Here again, let me offer y'all a little help. The sooner we leave, the better. If we wait, for example, until June or July, we run the risk of navigating the most rugged section of the trail in a blizzard. So what do you say?"

The class shouted, "April! April!"

As she made her selection, Mrs. Summerfield responded approvingly, "Okay, okay. So April it is."

The next screen appeared: "Before leaving Independence, you should buy equipment and supplies. You have $1,600 in cash, but you don't have to spend it all now. You can buy whatever you need at Matt's General Store." With so much money burning holes in our pockets, we went on a spending spree, buying nine yokes of oxen, two thousand pounds of food, fourteen sets of clothing, twenty boxes of ammunition, and a host of miscellaneous wagon parts, including nine axles, wheels, and tongues. When all was said and done, we had invested a little over a thousand dollars of our funds, thus leaving us with a little less than six hundred for a rainy day.

After choosing a "grueling" rather than a "steady" or "strenuous" pace and selecting a "filling" over a "meager" or "adequate" diet, we eagerly set out from Independence on April 1, 1848. But excitement quickly turned to nail biting. The first leg of our journey was anything but auspicious. Before even reaching our first milestone, the Kansas River Crossing at the one-hundred-and-two-mile mark, we had broken an axle; one of the oxen had injured a leg; the Duchess had come down with the measles; and poor Uncle Billy had contracted cholera! But we adventurers soldiered on, ferrying across the Kansas River; floating our wagon across the Big Blue; traveling one hundred eighty-five miles; and reaching Nebraska in ten days.

Mrs. Summerfield stepped away from the computer and said, "Class, check your textbooks. What is the next landmark on the trail? And how far is it from the Big Blue River? Anyone?" She scanned the room. "Okay, Janice, the next landmark and the distance to it?"

"Fort Kearny, Mrs. Summerfield. One hundred nineteen miles from the Big Blue."

"Very good. And can anyone tell us something about this particular fort's history?" Stats shot his hand into the air. "Okay, Kevin. What about this outpost? Where is it located? When was it established?"

"The fort's located in south central Nebraska near the Platte River. The US Army built the garrison in 1848. It served as a way station on the eastern part of the trail for prospectors and emigrants traveling westward to California and Oregon. It would have been the settlers' first chance to restock their food supplies. The fort's commanding officer was authorized to sell food and equipment to the settlers for cheap. And if the travelers were poor enough, he could give them the supplies for free."

As she moved back to the computer, Mrs. Summerfield nodded and said, "Very good, Kevin. And now, on with our journey!"

When she advanced the screen, the game advised us, "From Fort Kearny it is 250 miles to Chimney Rock." Mrs. Summerfield asked, "So can someone tell us where the rock's located and give us a description?" She paused. "All right, I see a hand in the back of the room there. Bobby?"

"Ah, it's in western Nebraska... and, ah... ah..."

"And what *is* Chimney Rock? Feel free to refer to your textbook and notes, Bobby."

He looked down at his notebook and read the description he had copied out of his textbook the night before: "Chimney Rock is a three-hundred-foot natural spire composed of sandstone, clay, and volcanic ash. It was made by the erosion of the cliffs at the edge of the North Platte Valley."

"That's right. This mound of earth with a tower stuck on top was the most famous landmark on the Oregon Trail. Since it could be seen for miles around, settlers always kept an eye out for it after leaving Fort Kearny." Mrs. Summerfield paused briefly to consult her notes and then continued. "The game summary says we've been on the road for three weeks now and we've traveled five hundred fifty-four miles. We have an opportunity to hunt for food. What do you think? Wanna do some hunting?"

The class erupted, "Yes! Yes!"

Mrs. Summerfield made her selection and read the hunting instructions aloud. She informed us she would be the hunter for our party that day. "Hit *Return Key* to start or stop walking, *Arrow Keys* to point the rifle, and *Space Bar* to fire the rifle." She took a deep breath, hit the space bar to advance the screen, and said, "Well… here goes nothing."

And there she was, poor Mrs. Summerfield, standing alone in a field dotted with boulders. A deer raced across the screen. She shot some five yards behind her prey. Two rabbits appeared from either side of the screen. She fired at the one to her right and missed badly. She swung around, shot and killed the other rabbit with a lucky shot. The class cheered! Next a squirrel tried sneaking across the bottom of the screen. Mrs. Summerfield fired two shots, missing badly with both. But as with the rabbit, she finally nailed the squirrel with a lucky third shot. No time to relax, though. Another squirrel appeared and scooted across the screen from left to right. Our fearless hunter fired twice and didn't even come close. And then a screen popped up indicating the hunting trip was over. The text box informed us, "From the animals you shot, you got only five pounds of meat."

Mrs. Summerfield, sensing Stats was mocking her marksmanship, rushed to the back of the room, towered over his desk, and said good-naturedly, "Okay, Kevin, if you think you can do any better, step right up there to the computer and strut your stuff." Kevin acted decisively. He jumped up, ran to the front of the room, and chose "Hunt for food" on the menu.

Now it was Stats's turn to stand in the field of boulders and try replenishing our supplies. The pressure was really on now. A deer appeared and disappeared before Stats could get off a shot. Next a buffalo lumbered in from screen right. Stats fired once, twice, three times, and then felled the buffalo with a fourth shot. The class cheered! After two deer fell victim to our very own Leatherstocking, the screen popped up announcing the result of the hunt: "From the animals you shot, you got nine hundred fifty pounds of meat. However, you were only able to carry one hundred pounds back to the wagon." Our cheering at the total pounds Stats had amassed quickly turned to boos as we discovered we only netted ten percent of the total take.

Mrs. Summerfield returned to the front of the room and congratulated Stats on his hunting skills, asking, "So whenever we get low on food, whom do y'all want handling the rifle?" She smiled as she elicited the desired response from us: "Kevin! Kevin! Kevin!"

From Chimney Rock it was on to Fort Laramie, Wyoming; Soda Springs, Idaho; the Blue Mountains of northeastern Oregon; and then to the small frontier town of the Dalles some hundred miles or so from our final destination in the Willamette Valley. While we had all escaped with our lives so far, I couldn't say the trip from Fort Laramie to the Dalles was uneventful. Besides the heat, the rugged terrain, and the scarcity of water, injured animals and serious bouts of dysentery and typhoid fever plagued us almost every step of the way.

Mrs. Summerfield said, "So far, so good, but it's now decision time. We can take the new Barlow toll road over the Cascade Mountains, or we can follow Marcus Whitman's advice and take the wagon apart and float it down the dangerous Columbia River on a raft. What do you want to do?"

As soon as we heard the word *dangerous*, we all roared, "Take the river! Take the river!"

Mrs. Summerfield selected "Float down the Columbia River" from the menu options, and a set of navigational instructions appeared on the screen. "Use the arrow keys to guide the raft through the rushing waters of the Columbia River. After passing the third direction sign, land the raft at the trail to the Willamette Valley."

Mrs. Summerfield advanced the screen and our loaded raft floated out into the channel. Two boulders appeared downstream. Mrs. Summerfield started pounding the arrow keys, causing our raft to zigzag erratically from bank to bank. I had a sinking feeling (no pun intended) that her seamanship would prove inferior even to her marksmanship. But, by the grace of God, we managed somehow to sail between the boulders and past the first of the three direction signs. The class cheered!

As soon as the next boulders appeared at the left of the screen, Mrs. Summerfield started pounding the arrow keys again, sending us hurtling downstream from side to side as if participating in a highly competitive slalom race. Somehow we whizzed through the second set of boulders and raced past the second direction sign. The class cheered again!

A third boulder field appeared, and Mrs. Summerfield started pounding the arrow keys once again. Our goal, the land route just beyond the third direction sign, appeared at the far left of the screen. And for some inexplicable reason, I began to relax. Something said our chances of surviving were improving by the minute. We had momentum. We had already dodged the bullet twice. "God must be our copilot in this risky venture," I thought.

Mrs. Summerfield kept pounding, and the raft kept bounding from bank to bank. One more set of rocks to navigate and we'd be home. But only seconds later reasonable assumption crashed into jagged reality. We were tossed up onto the boulders. The class gasped. A message flashed on the screen: "Your raft has hit a rock! You have lost: Duchess (drowned); Uncle Billy (drowned); Piney Woods (drowned); Oakhurst (drowned); fourteen oxen; four sets of clothing; five hundred bullets; four wagon tongues; three wagon wheels; and six hundred pounds of food." This time all but four in the class served up a Bronx cheer.

I glanced over at Stats, Bones, and Zulu, who were staring somberly at the floor. The Outcasts of Poker Flats understood the implication. Unlike the initial hunting trip near Chimney Rock, there wouldn't be a do-over. Resurrection was not in the cards. And yes, the Outcasts also grasped the symbolism of a well-intentioned leader inadvertently casting her charges off into the depths.

A chagrined Mrs. Summerfield cleared her throat and asked, "Do you want to go on?"

Bradley shouted, "Yes! Yes! Not everyone's dead!"

The class laughed and cheered, "Go on! Go on!"

"Okay, then. It's on to the Willamette Valley! I see the trailhead just beyond the boulders there. Once we get by these rocks we'll be home free."

Ironically, her hand steadied and she eased past the final threats effortlessly, as if channeling Meriwether Lewis on his landmark expedition down the raging Columbia to the sea. She mumbled to herself, "Easy... easy there! Easy.... Terra firma!" And after a brief ride on the overland trail, the lone survivor finally reached her destination on June 30, 1848.

Mrs. Summerfield hit the space bar, and an intriguing ahistorical dialogue box appeared: "Congratulations! You have made it to Oregon! Let's see how many points you have earned." She eagerly tapped the space bar again, and up popped a scorecard. "Points for arriving in Oregon: one person in very poor health—200; one wagon—50; twelve oxen—48; eighteen spare wagon parts—36; twelve sets of clothing—24; fifty bullets—1; six hundred pounds of food—24; $525 in cash—105. Total = 488."

She advanced the screen and a provocative prompt said, "To see if you qualify for the Oregon Top Ten, please flip your diskette to side one."

The neurotypicals shouted encouragement. "Flip it! Flip it!" But their expectations were soon dashed. As the Top Ten list appeared with point totals approaching the eight thousand mark, our classmates groaned and accepted a resounding and final defeat. I say "final" because few of our peers ever ventured onto the Oregon Trail again. It was too much like work. They didn't buy Mrs. Summerfield's hype lifted straight from the packaging: "This will help y'all solve problems more quickly, increase your reading comprehension, develop your map-reading abilities, sharpen your survival skills, learn about western expansion and the settling of the Old West, and explore the geography of the United States."

As our classmates groused, I glanced over at Stats, Bones, and Zulu. They had buried their faces in their hands again, fighting hard to hide the grins. None of us Outcasts wanted our smiles misinterpreted as blatant signs of schadenfreude. Our joy and excitement had nothing to do with our classmates' failure to excel at *The Oregon Trail*. Instead, it had everything to do with recognizing an opportunity to strengthen the bond between us Outcasts through daily doses of cyber competition.

As with many life-altering events, we couldn't see much beyond our middle school horizons. We realized Mrs. Summerfield had introduced us to an engaging source of friendly competition and knew *The Oregon Trail* would soon appear on at least four wish lists for the upcoming holidays. It would only be years later in replaying our careers that we would truly come to understand the significance of that teacher, that assignment, that lab, that game on that cold, bright December day.

Stats downed the rest of his beer in one draft, shook his head, and said, "How'd we miss it, Casey J.? It was as plain as the nose on your face. The assignment. Remember the homework assignment?"

We were sitting in a bar just off the Pantheon campus, catching up after an absence of some ten years. We had been through many highs and lows together since fifth-grade social studies, but it was clear that day had stayed with both of us through all of it.

"Yeah, vaguely. I know it had something to do with settling the West and traveling the Oregon Trail."

"That's right. Do ya remember the lesson title?"

I shook my head. "No. I'll have to rely on you for that one."

Stats smiled and proudly proclaimed, "Expansion and Manifest Destiny. Just think of it! Now how ironic is that? Yeah, old Mrs. Summerfield was talking about the country without ever realizing she was playing a decisive role in our growth—and you might say even in our fate."

I laughed. "It's funny, Stats, how when you get to thinking back, how things seem to pop into your head."

"Like what?"

"The children's proverb about the lost nail. You know:

For want of a nail the shoe was lost.
For want of a shoe the horse was lost.
For want of a horse the knight was lost.
For want of a knight the message was lost.
For want of a message the battle was lost.
For want of a battle the kingdom was lost.
And all for the want of a horseshoe nail.

"Yeah, I remember the rhyme. What about it?"

"I dunno. I never thought of these words specifically—you know, back then in middle school, high school, or even in college—but I sure had the feeling."

69

"The feeling?"

"Yeah. As kids, I just sensed the kingdom was already lost. I never said anything to anybody. And I tried fighting it every day. Did you ever feel it was hopeless, Stats?"

"Yeah. It was tough getting knocked down every day and finding the guts to get back up and keep on going. And now that you put it that way—I mean about the nail—I guess I did sense something vital was missing and, yes, the kingdom had already been lost. But on that day in the lab, Casey J., we Outcasts found the nail, didn't we?"

I nodded and raised my glass, "Yeah, Stats. We sure did. We found the nail that day."

5

I SLAMMED THE RECEIVER DOWN when I heard the supervisor say to Mama, "Excuse me, ma'am, the fellows want to know what to do with all the unpacked equipment stacked in the bedroom upstairs." I raced up to the landing where Bluto was standing holding one of my prized SEs by the scruff of its neck. I extended my arms and approached warily as if trying to talk the brute and his hostage down off a ledge. I slid my hands slowly beneath the case and said as calmly as I could, "Here, sir, let me help you with that. We'll be taking all the electronics over to the new place ourselves in our pickup."

Moving out of our parents' homes into a rented house near the Pantheon campus was Bones's idea. After she broached the subject at one of our daily competitions, Zulu pushed back hard. "So how are we going to get past the requirement that all incoming freshmen have to live on campus?"

"It'll take a little doing," Bones replied, "but I have a plan."

"Okay, then. We're all ears," Zulu said.

"Well, first of all we'll have to get requests for waivers from our shrinks."

"Based on what?" I asked.

"Based on our anticipated difficulties living in the dorms, being squeezed into tight spaces with two or three classmates."

"But, Bones, you're forgetting one critical element here."

"Yeah? What's that, Casey J.?"

"Our folks. They'll be footing the bill, you know."

"Yeah, I know," she hurried to explain. "But no worries. I've already thought that through. In fact, it's the easiest piece of the puzzle."

"How's that?" Zulu asked.

"Once the white coats get on board they'll convince the parents it's the right thing to do. *Capiche*?"

Zulu nodded and muttered, "Yeah, yeah. We get it. But it still seems like a lot of work."

"That's true until you consider the alternative," said Bones, "living in the dorm with a bunch of jerks who don't get you. Who'll ignore you unless they need something from you, making fun of you all the time behind your back."

I jumped in. "And, Zulu, you have to consider the upside too. There'll be classes in the morning. Next it's back to the house for lunch. Then hit the games early afternoon, pause for dinner, back to the games, and then finish off the day with a little homework or some studying for an exam. It'll be nirvana!"

Stats jumped in. "Hey, Zulu, the bases are loaded and no outs! Sure sounds a lot like a plan to me. Count me in!"

"Me too!" I proclaimed.

"That makes three!" Bones exclaimed. "So what about you, Zulu?"

We turned and focused on our Doubting Thomas who had in fact already begun nodding. "Yeah, count me in too."

Mama and I followed the moving van over to the historic Thunderwood district of McGill on the north side of the Pantheon campus. According to legend, the Chickasaws migrated eastward during the Middle Ages. Every night of the journey, their priests would set a pole in the ground vertically, and when the tribe awoke the following morning, they would migrate that day in the direction the pole was leaning. It always pointed east, that is, until one morning they awoke and the marker was standing upright, which meant they had finally arrived at their new home in what is now McGill's Thunderwood district.

After great rejoicing, the tribe cleared the forests, planted corn, and set about establishing their community. At the end of that first growing season, the Chickasaws celebrated with a traditional green corn ceremony. While men scoured the forest for charred but living trees struck by lightning, the women prepared a pit for this "thunderwood," which would soon fuel the sacred fire within the sacred circle. Three long wails announced the beginning of the celebration—and then began the deep vibration of drums and the rattle of gourds, the swaying of men and trees, silent prayers to the Thunder Beings, and finally whoops of survival, renewal, and redemptive joy.

We turned onto tree-lined Jackson Avenue and rolled to a stop in front of a "lovingly restored" turn-of-the-century Craftsman bungalow. The simple mahogany, two-story structure was set back some seventy-five feet from the road and was framed by a refined setting of hydrangea, azalea, dogwood, and evergreen. This unadorned beauty harmonized effort-lessly with its surroundings. The materials used to craft it had been left in their natural state. The exterior walls were shingled. The foundation and the broad chimney facing the street were made from cobblestones. Adding to this sense of oneness with the environment were the front wraparound and rear screened porches where you could sidle up to the landscape and com-mune with nature.

The front entrance opened up directly into the living room, which was separated from the kitchen/dining area by a half wall. The most dramatic aspect of the living room (and of the house overall, for that matter) was the massive Arts and Crafts fireplace and mantel made of clinker bricks, which had been discarded earlier because of their distortion and discoloration. But we all know one man's trash is another's treasure. And the odd, irreg-ular shapes and colors of these rejected bricks screamed rebellion against the sterile uniformity of machine-made building supplies that had begun to dominate architecture at the end of the 1800s.

While the main level featured an open floor plan, the upstairs was divided into four bedrooms and a bath. Each of the bedrooms offered an inviting built-in window bench ideal for reading or admiring the landscape below. Walnut-stained trim, beams, and floors were juxtaposed with plaster walls and ceilings throughout the house. Other Arts and Crafts high-lights included stained and leaded glass and six-over-one, dou-ble-hung windows, allowing an abundance of natural light to bathe every nook and cranny of the new Outcast Headquarters.

Zulu, Bones, and I awoke on the first day of classes to our designated alarm pounding on a saucepan with a spoon and shouting, "It's game day, y'all! It's game day! First time up in the majors! All you rookies out here now, with your game faces on!"

One after the other we stumbled down the stairs to the kitchen where Stats greeted us with orange juice, single-serving boxes of cereal, and an irritatingly enthusiastic game plan. "Bones, your cornflakes are over there. Zulu, your shredded wheat is here. Casey J., your cocoa squares are there next to Bones. And—ta-da!—my snap crackles are right here at the head of the table. Once we've chowed down, we'll hurry over to the Haldeman Arch before classes begin."

Zulu interrupted, "The Haldeman Arch?"

Stats nodded. "Yeah, the gateway to the campus. Been there well over a hundred years."

"So am I missing something here? We have to head over to this arch before going to classes?"

"Yeah, Zulu, it'll bring us good luck. My father told me about it last spring. He was a student here eons ago. Says it's tradition."

Zulu continued probing. "Tradition? Tradition to do what? Skip under the arch, and it'll bring us good luck?"

"Come on now, Zulu. It's a little more than skipping under the arch."

"So what are we supposed to do then to have some good luck for a change?"

Stats pounded the table. "Okay, everyone, get your faces out of your cereal and listen up. You have to follow tradition to a T if you want this to work. Y'all ready? Okay, then. First, you place your right hand over the word *Fidelis*, carved in the right support pillar. Next, you place your right hand across your heart; and then you touch the Latin inscription again. My father vows if we swear allegiance to a new *Alma Mater Studiorum*, we're sure to have academic success."

Stats paused to take several bites of his snap crackles and then continued laying out the rest of our day. "After visiting the arch, we'll head over to Redman Hall for Computer Science. We'll split up for our electives, and when we're all finished, we'll meet up again at the arch at, let's say, thirteen hundred hours. We should all be done with our classes by then."

I jumped in. "Why backtracking to the arch, Stats? That's going the wrong way, going away from home."

He smiled broadly and wagged his index finger. "That would be right, if yours truly didn't have a little surprise in store for his compatriots this afternoon."

"Ooh, a surprise. What is it?" Bones asked.

Stats laughed, continuing to hold his cards close to his vest. "Ask me no questions, and I'll tell y'all no lies. All I'll say is that after we're finished with our surprise, we'll then head back here and fire up the desktops for some *Harrier Strike Mission* sorties before getting down to homework."

Bones interrupted. "Okay by me, as long as we get in some *Dark Knight* too. Remember, it's Friday the thirteenth, which means the Great Hall will be decorated just for today."

"How could we ever forget that Easter egg, Bones?" Stats said. "You remind us every Christmas and Friday the thirteenth about the Great Hall or the throne room being decked out in holiday decorations."

"I dunno. I just think it's neat," Bones said defensively.

"Yeah… 'neat' is the right word for it. But honestly it's not in the same league with the guys who buried a flight simulator in Excel and a game of pinball in Word. Now those eggs, my friend, are way beyond neat. They're just flat-out cool!"

I glanced at my watch and sounded the alarm. "If we're gonna stop by the arch before the circus starts, we've got to get to humping. We have a little over thirty minutes until showtime."

The four of us finished up our cereal, rinsed out our bowls, and gathered our bags for the first day of what would prove to be a game-changing school year.

At the prescribed thirteen hundred hours three of the four Outcasts paced beneath the Haldeman Arch trying to spot our fearless leader, the master of surprises, who, as usual, was missing in action. Zulu groused, "You'd think someone so good at math could do a little better when it comes to time. After all, it's numbers, for God's sake."

"Cut him some slack, Zulu," I said. "He had the farthest to walk. His algorithm class was way over on the northeast corner of the quadrangle near the Student Union."

"Well, I'm just saying."

"There he is!" Bones shouted. "See him?"

"Where?" Zulu demanded.

"If you'd put your glasses on, you'd see him. He's right there, running. He just passed the fountain. See him?"

Zulu peered toward the center of the quadrangle. "Yeah, yeah. Okay. I see him now. I can't wait to hear his excuse this time."

As Stats approached, we could hear him shouting his apology. "Sorry, guys! Sorry!" He stopped beneath the arch, shed his backpack, and put his hands on his knees trying to catch his breath.

Despite our admonition, Zulu played the bad cop. "Hey, Superman, you gonna blame it on kryptonite this time?"

Stats looked up and scowled, "No! Karatsuba multiplication."

"Kara what?"

"Karatsuba multiplication…. Hang on, let me catch my breath." Stats stood upright and took a deep breath before explaining. "Toward the end of class the TA was trying to explain Karatsuba. All he really had to say was 'he was a Soviet mathematician who in 1962 discovered a faster way of multiplying large integers. The running time for his algorithm grows like $n^{\log 3} \approx n^{1.58}$.' That's all he had to say. It's really pretty simple. But he just kept droning on as the clock ticked down toward thirteen hundred hours."

"Whatever," Zulu muttered.

Sensing he had successfully blunted Zulu's frontal assault, Stats donned his backpack and said cagily, "Okay, Outcasts, fall in line and follow me for the treat of a lifetime!"

6

W E EXITED THE QUADRANGLE through the storied arch and began walking west on Main. As we approached the second light, Stats slowed and morphed into a guide. "Some folks call this intersection here the 'Death Spiral.'" He paused long enough to set the hook and then added, "You have to think of it as the unwinding of a life. Beginning there on the northeast corner and moving counterclockwise you first see the Medical Arts Building overflowing with obstetricians, pediatricians, internists, and specialists. On the northwest corner, you have the McGill General Hospital. Then after crossing the street, you find the Patrick Mortuary on the southwest corner. And completing the cycle we find Solley's Flower Station at the southeast corner of Beauregard and Main."

While waiting for the light at this metaphorically charged intersection, Stats pointed in the direction of Solley's and said, "We're going right over there for lunch. My father's treat in honor of our first day of classes."

Zulu leaned in and whispered snidely, "Eating at the flower shop? We're all herbivores?"

Never at a loss for words or hearing acuity, Stats retorted, "That's right, Zu. While the rest of us are over there enjoying our rose hips, you'll be dining on thorns!"

"You're just too funny for—"

I jumped in to end the joust. "Seriously, Stats, where are we headed?"

He smiled and responded with a riddle. "Your choice, Casey J. We can turn onto Beauregard or continue on up Main."

"Choice of restaurants?"

"No, choice of entrances."

"How's that?"

"Two entrances to the restaurant surrounding Solley's—one on Beauregard and the other on Main. Y'all are gonna like this place. The food's good, and it puts the lie to Shakespeare's assertion 'that which we call a rose / By any other name would smell as sweet.'"

Our quizzical expressions egged Stats on. "The establishment's had a lot of names, looks, and owners over the years, but the downhome cooking's never changed. I know it sounds strange, but every time new owners come in, they change the names of the items on the menu but they never futz around with the recipes. They don't need to. The originals are downright good. The menu goes all the way back to the first eatery at the corner. The original owner, a retired lawyer, tried extending the life cycle metaphor beyond the four corners, first calling his place Probate and then Executor. But when he got wind his patrons enjoyed the joke but loathed the legalese, he found a way to extend the metaphor without offending his clientele."

"How'd he thread the needle, Stats?" I asked.

"He used his own first name. The Executor simply became Will's."

"Clever. So I guess where there's a will there's a way, huh?"

Bones groaned. "Stop it with the puns, you two! They're killing me!"

"You haven't heard the half of it," Stats said, laughing. "After several years, Will decided to hang it up for good and retire to Boca Raton. He sold the place to a surveillance company CEO who renamed the restaurant the Two-Way Café."

"Because he sold security mirrors?" Bones asked.

"Close but no cigar. And you're not in bad company, Bones. About half the townspeople have speculated his glass business inspired the name."

"What about the other half? What do they think was the origin?" Zulu probed.

"Uh, it's a bit more complicated. The other half believes the name has sexual connotations."

"And? Spell it out."

"Well, the other half mistakenly thinks it has to do with bisexuality."

"So if a hundred percent are wrong, what's the real answer then?" I asked. "Must be something pretty esoteric."

Stats laughed. "Yeah, really deep. Like naming his acquisition the Two-Way Café because it had two entrances. It was as simple as that."

The three of us groaned loudly, which only encouraged Stats to continue his oral history. "Well, after thirty-five years, the surveillance entrepreneur sold the restaurant to a libertarian, who played off those who believed the Two-Way had something to do with sex."

"What'd he do?" Zulu asked.

Stats laughed. "Y'all ready for this?"

In unison we cringed but urged him on, "Yeah, yeah. Keep going!"

"The libertarian just went with the flow. If you can't fight 'em, you join 'em. So he changed the name from the Two-Way to the Anyway Café!"

"You know this is actually getting pretty funny, Stats," I said. "You got any other owners you want to tell us about?"

I could sense Stats was relishing every minute of our exchange. He was smiling, wringing his hands, and silently praying we'd be asking for more. "As a matter of fact, the place has seen more hands than a high-stakes poker dealer."

It was now Bones's turn to advance the discussion. "So tell us, Stats, who was next in the long line of owners?"

"Juliet Harris," he replied. "She was a college professor of film and theater. She bought the restaurant from the libertarian. And to increase business she added a vintage wine bar and showcased classic foreign films on weekends. You know, like Fellini, Cocteau, Kurosawa, Tarkovsky, Ber."

Zulu jumped in. "Don't tell us. She changed the name again, right?"

Stats beamed. "She sure did. So do we have any takers here about the new name?"

I shook my head and responded, "The professor's better than I am if she came up with a catchy phrase connecting the wine and the movies."

Stats laughed aloud. "Oh, she did you even one better. She connected all the dots—the bar, the movies, and her own name!"

"Okay, Stats. What'd she call the place this time?" Zulu asked impatiently.

"Y'all won't believe it. May we have a drum roll please?" We obliged and Stats announced, "The professor called her restaurant Juliet of the Spirits!"

We just stood there grinning and shaking our heads as the traffic light changed to red for a third time.

"So are we eating at Juliet's today?" Bones asked.

Stats smiled and replied, "You're getting closer, but we're not there yet."

"You mean the restaurant changed hands again?"

Stats nodded. "Yeah. Professor Harris sold the place to an actor who kept the restaurant and wine bar intact but converted the entertainment from foreign films to live standup comedy."

"And hilarity ensued," I said.

"Unbelievable!" Stats exclaimed. "That's unbelievable! You got it in one!"

"Got what?" I asked.

"The name," he replied.

"The name?"

"Yeah, that's what the actor called his restaurant–comedy club. And Hilarity Ensued."

I laughed and shrugged, "Do I get some sort of prize?"

Stats was ready with a rejoinder. "Congrats, Casey J. You've won a free lunch at the…"

"Hilarity Ensued?" I asked.

Stats shook his head. "No, but we're almost there."

Bones picked up the narrative. "So the actor sold the place to… ?"

"To a shady operator rumored to have ties to the Chicago underworld."

Zulu began singing softly, "Look what they've done to my song, Ma."

Bones interrupted. "Comedy and the mafia, now that's a stretch!"

"Yeah, for sure. The buyer knew that'd be a bridge too far."

"So what he do?" I asked.

"Kept the restaurant, the booze, and the live entertainment."

Zulu probed. "So what changed?"

"Ah, the type of acts, the clientele, and the name of the place."

"So lay it on us, Stats. What exactly did the buyer do?"

"He converted 'Hilarity Ensued' into a gentleman's club. Live burlesque. But upscale, not the sleaze." He paused to set another hook and asked, "Any takers on the new name?"

We all shrugged.

"NSFW!" Stats proclaimed. "Clever, huh? NSFW!"

We shook our heads and laughed.

Zulu jumped in, "So your father's footing the bill today for lunch at the gentleman's club? That's weird, Stats!"

"Yeah, weird if it were true. But we're not headed over to NSFW for lunch. Let's cross the street now, read the latest sign, and find out where we're eating."

When the light changed for the fifth time, we crossed the intersection, turned on to Beauregard, and stopped outside the restaurant. "Well, here we are!" Stats said.

I scanned the front of the building and replied, "You told us we'd read the latest sign here. There's nothing but the address—70."

"Look carefully, Casey J. You're right, it's the address. But you see the point between the numbers? It's the 7.0, meaning this is the seventh iteration of a restaurant at this location."

"Clever," I muttered.

Stats opened the door and motioned for us to enter. "Wait till you see the inside. The 7.0 has a lot more to say about the décor and theme of the café than the number of establishments that have operated here over the years." As we passed through a narrow hallway, Stats pointed to signage above the doorway leading into the dining area and then added, "So there's your first clue to the relationship between the 7.0, the décor, and the overall theme. The sign says we're entering 'The Digital Divide.'"

And indeed the dining room was divided into two sections, with one area containing what appeared to be a random mixture of eight round and rectangular tables while the second area was comprised solely of circular tables. I asked Zulu and Bones, "Y'all see any clues in the layout there?"

Bones began analyzing the scene aloud. "Well, I see a jumble of round and rectangular tables in one of the two seating areas. No logical pattern. And there seem to be more circular tables in both sections. Five in the first one there and all eight circular in the second area."

"Time for a clue?" Stats asked, practically vibrating with excitement.

We nodded.

He responded, "Bits and bytes."

The three of us game-show contestants looked at each other and repeated, "Bits and bytes. Hmm… bits and bytes."

Bones shouted, "Got it! The layout depicts a base-two number system. The dining room's binary. See? The circular tables are zeroes; the rectangular tables are ones."

After sharing a laugh with my compatriots, I entered the analytic fray. "Stats's clue was bits *and* bytes. I forget. How many bits to a byte?"

"Eight!" Zulu shouted.

"Okay, we have sixteen tables divided into two sections of eight each. So we have two bytes here. Let's see, the first byte, if you will, contains five zeroes and three ones. The second has nothing but zeroes. That's the pattern. But I don't know how to count it out in binary without a reference. Either of you know?"

Bones and Zulu shook their heads.

"It's seventy!" Stats shouted. "It's binary for seventy. The restaurant's address!"

The awestruck chorus chimed in admiringly one after another. "Sweet!" "Awesome!" "Good one!"

And the digital layout was only the first example of the link between décor and a futuristic theme. Each of the sections featured a wall-mounted widescreen television with one streaming live broadcasts of TechTV and a second looping taped episodes of *Nerds 2.0.1*. The dining area had a minimalist feel with smooth concrete floors and recessed industrial metal ceiling lamps, creating a linear "memory socket" effect throughout the space. The brushed-chrome dining tables were topped with butcher block, equipped with hidden surge protectors, and flanked by black leather and chrome seating.

A robotic greeter approached, and without lifting his eyes from his wireless PDA, he said in a soft, calm, HAL 9000 voice, "Good afternoon. Export or import?"

As a returning customer, Stats took the lead. "Good afternoon. We're importing today. May we have a 'one' for four by the windows in the '7 byte,' please?"

"Follow me."

After weaving our way through a labyrinth of headphones, laptops, and derivative calculators, we arrived at a rectangular table in the "7" section. As the greeter input our table location into his palmtop, he said, "Please be seated. Here are the protocols. Your compiler will be around in a nanosecond to discuss today's specials and take your commands."

I leaned in and whispered, "Looks like you'll be in charge of decoding this afternoon, Stats."

"No problem," he said, adding, "but it won't take y'all long to get the hang of the lingo. You'll see."

And within sixty billion nanoseconds, a tall, bearded, bespectacled waiter appeared and said, "Good afternoon. My name is Stuart. I'll be your compiler today. Before we get started, I'd like to query, any of you programmed here before?"

Stats nodded and replied, "Yeah, I have several times. But my friends here haven't been in before. I'll be playing the kernel today."

"Roger that," the waiter said as he whipped a PDA out of his back pocket. "Okay, then. Today's Trojan Horse is the phish and chips. And as you know you can ROM or RAM."

"I'll stick to ROM today," Stats said.

"Very good then. So for booting up… what'll it be?"

"The Handler."

"Bits and bytes?" he asked.

"Sure, why not?" Stats answered.

"Next?"

"Spaghetti Code."

"Megahertz?"

"Absolutely."

"Anything else?"

"A bundle."

"How would you like that done? Stock or overclocked?"

"Overclocked," Stats said.

"Expanded or compressed?"

"Expanded. The bells and whistles."

"Backend application?"

"What do we have today?" Stats asked.

"Cookies and Drive Surprise."

Stats smiled. "Okay. I'll bite."

"Floppy or hard?"

"Floppy for me."

"To drink?"

"Java straight."

"Mega or gig?"

"Make it a gig."

The waiter surveyed the rest of us and asked, "Okay, whose next?"

Sensing the ladies were as lost as I was, I jumped in. "We'll all be having what he's having."

"Very well then. I'll put your commands in and loop back shortly with your java."

Zulu glanced over at Bones, shook her head, and then stared at Stats and me. "We know it's a freebie today, but what did you guys just order us up for lunch?"

I shrugged and laughed, "Hell if I know. We'll have to consult the expert here. I was a lost ball in high weeds when we got to ROM and RAM."

Stats raised his hands in a T and shouted, "Time out! Listen up! The waiter was asking whether I would be selecting items right off the menu—ROM—or making special requests via the restaurant's random access meal program—RAM."

"You went with the ROM, didn't you?" Bones asked.

"That's right and for starters I ordered a Handler with bits and bytes."

"And what is that exactly?" Zulu asked.

"Well, see if you can figure it out. I ordered a Secure Public Internet Access Handler… or a Handler for short."

After repeating the phrase several times, Bones shouted, "I get it! That's pretty funny, Stats."

"Excuse me, y'all mind cluing Zulu and me in on the joke?" I asked.

Bones laughed aloud before explaining. "Take the first letters of the words: the Secure Public Internet Access Handler. What do you get?"

I started muttering, "Let's see. S-P-I-"

Zulu and I exclaimed simultaneously, "Spinach!"

"Bravo!" Stats shouted. "That's right. I ordered a spinach salad with bacon bits and croutons."

"So what's on tap after our spinach salads, Stats?" I asked.

"Well, let's see. Next you'll be chowing down on a bowl of five-way, three-alarm chili, followed by a double cheeseburger—well done and fully dressed—and for dessert, the pièce de résistance, soft-serve ice cream, chocolate chip cookies, and a large coffee refill."

"You did good today, Stats," I said. "I mean bringing us here. This is really our kind of place!"

"I thought you guys would like the atmosphere. The food's really good too… and there's plenty of it. You'll see. You'll be running a backup for sure."

"Asking for doggie bags?" Bones asked.

Stats nodded. "Yeah, and see there? I told you it wouldn't take you long to get the hang of the lingo."

At that point Stuart returned with our drinks and announced, "Four gig of Java with Handlers on deck!"

As we raised our cups, Stats invoked an old Japanese proverb for a hopeful, defiant toast: "Fall seven times, stand up eight!"

7

THE RENOWNED PROFESSOR MORTON strode into the hall, deposited a stack of notebooks on the lectern, and peered out over his bifocals with a scowl. "I hope today's class goes a little better than last Friday's cluster. You'd all been forewarned to read the *entire* novel *before* our first meeting; and when I started drilling down into the last half of the work, it soon became clear the only people who had completed the assignment were the only two undeclared literature majors we have in the room, Sandra and Jason here. So I hope the weekend reprieve has given y'all sufficient time to redeem yourselves. But time will tell."

The professor paused to consult his notes and establish a boundary between an imperfect past and a hopeful future. He stroked his graying beard, scanned the hall, and asked, "How's this particular course listed in the undergraduate bulletin?" He peered at us. "Oh, come on now. It's not a trick question. Anyone?" Silence. "Okay, I see a hand way up there in the back. So the bulletin says… ?"

The rafters responded, "Writing the Contemporary World: Saying No! in Thunder."

"That's right, and according to the bulletin, which contemporary writers are on the menu this semester?" He peered around again at the silent room. "Come on now. Don't be bashful. Y'all know what you've signed up for.… Okay, we have a brave soul over there. So, David, who are the writers we'll be exploring this semester?"

"Powers, Pynchon, and, ah, Peixoto."

"Yes. And any ideas why we'd be reading a nineteenth-century novel right out of the box in a contemporary literature course? Anyone? No takers? Okay, then, let's take it from the top." The professor cleared his throat and launched his formal lecture. "In a letter to Hawthorne after completing *Moby-Dick* Melville writes: 'A sense of unspeakable security is in me this moment, on account of your having understood the book. I have written a wicked book, and feel spotless as the lamb.' But written a book for whom? The general public?"

The class shook its head and mumbled, "No?"

"Well then, for whom was he writing? Do I see a hand? Anyone?"

I raised my hand, and the professor called on me. "So, Jason, for whom was he writing?"

"For all of us wanderers… outcasts… seekers living then and now."

"Interesting take, Jason. Can you support your assertion?"

I nodded and quickly checked my notes. "Yes, in chapter seventy-nine, I believe Melville prophesies. He says: 'If hereafter any highly cultured, poetical nation shall lure back to their birth-right, the merry May-day gods of old,… the great

Sperm Whale shall lord it.' I believe Melville was looking well beyond his death and envisioning *Moby-Dick* lording it over other nineteenth-century rivals."

"If you're correct, Jason, then Melville's prediction played out in spades. But it would be another thirty years after his death before the Melville revival would begin in earnest with Weaver's biography declaring, 'Being of sane intellect, that since letters began there never was such a book [as *Moby-Dick*], and that the mind of man is not constructed so as to produce such another; that I put its author with Rabelais, Swift and Shakespeare.'

"So why read Melville here in this particular contemporary comparative lit class?" He paused briefly for effect before again answering his own question. "First, because of the biographical similarities between Melville and our three contemporary novelists currently under review. As Melville before them, none has been afraid to challenge his readers with difficult material."

Professor Morton referred to his notes and transitioned to his next point. "So let's now talk a little about approach and structure. A question for y'all: Is *Moby-Dick* a straight-line, seafaring narrative?"

In unison the class responded with a muffled, "No."

"But on the surface it seems to be. You have a bunch of folks boarding a ship headed for the South Pacific. The monomaniacal sea captain seeks revenge on a specific whale that has maimed him in the past. The seamen find the whale. A struggle ensues. Leviathan wins. And a sole survivor shares his story. Sounds pretty straightforward to me. Where am I going wrong? Anyone?"

Mark, a student sitting two rows over from me, answered. I recognized him as a pretty sharp kid from one of my other classes. "The research 'Extracts' before the first chapter hint at many of the wide-ranging subjects Melville would weave into his novel."

"Can you name a few for us?"

"Let's see. There's history, religion, literature, music, philosophy, zoology, geology, mathematics…"

"But science?"

"Yes, sir. Chapter thirty-two, for example, is a lengthy treatise on cetology."

"Okay. I'll buy your science, but isn't mathematics a stretch? Anyone support Mark here? Anyone else see math in *Moby-Dick*?"

Bones's hand immediately shot into the air.

"Sandra, you agree with Mark that you can find mathematical references in *Moby-Dick*?"

"Yes, sir. After I saw the first one, I started jotting them down. You see, Casey J., ah, Jason here and I, we have a friend who's really into math. I thought he'd find the references fascinating."

"I see. So tell us what you found."

Bones glanced at her notebook. "In chapter seventy-four," she began, "during a discussion of the whale having eyes on opposite sides of its head, Melville alludes to Euclid and congruity. In chapter eighty it's squaring the circle. In chapter ninety-six it's what our friend Stats described as the tautochrone problem. In chapter—"

Professor Morton raised his hand signaling Bones had more than proven her point. He asked the class, "So everyone's on board with Mark and Sandra that we have something more than a straight-line sea-faring narrative here?"

The class nodded and answered boldly, "Yes!"

The professor smiled and said, "Well, I'm happy to report Melville agrees with your assessment. So, Mark, why don't you read aloud the third paragraph of chapter one hundred and four, 'The Fossil Whale,' which begins, 'One often hears of writers…'"

Mark thumbed through his copy and started reading:

> One often hears of writers that rise and swell
> with their subject, though it may seem but an
> ordinary one. How, then, with me, writing
> of this Leviathan? Unconsciously my chirog-
> raphy expands into placard capitals. Give me
> a condor's quill! Give me Vesuvius' crater for
> an inkstand! Friends, hold my arms! For in
> the mere act of penning my thoughts of this
> Leviathan, they weary me, and make me faint
> with their outreaching comprehensiveness of
> sweep, as if to include the whole circle of the
> sciences, and all the generations of whales,
> and men, and mastodons, past, present, and
> to come, with all the revolving panoramas of

empire on earth, and throughout the whole
universe, not excluding its suburbs.

The professor interrupted. "Thanks, Mark. Let's stop there for a minute to ask an inconvenient question. Why would Melville junk up a straightforward narrative by throwing in everything including the kitchen sink?"

Bones's arm shot up again to muffled groans scattered about the room.

"Okay, Sandra, can you help us with this conundrum?"

She answered confidently, "You must think of the narrative as a skeleton on which Melville applies the muscle."

"A very good analogy, Sandra, and I think Melville would totally agree. But why does he need all this bone and muscle? Anyone?... No?... Mark, why don't you pick up now where you left off."

Our classmate nodded and continued reading: "'Such, and so magnifying, is the virtue of a large and liberal theme! We expand to its bulk. To produce a mighty book, you must choose a mighty theme. No great and enduring volume can ever be written on the flea, though many there be who have tried it.'"

"Thanks, Mark. We'll stop there." Professor Morton scanned the room. "So what is Melville's explanation for all the apparent digressions? Well, borrowing Sandra's terminology for a moment, the 'skeletal' sea-faring narrative supports the historical, philosophical, scientific 'muscle,' which in turn informs and reinforces 'a mighty theme.'"

"So why read Melville here in this particular class? Well, first, as we said, because of the biographical similarities between Melville and our three contemporary novelists, and second because of the similarities in their approaches." Professor Morton referred to his notes before speaking again. "There is one more point I'd like to make. In our remaining time today let's talk about that 'mighty theme' that Melville mentions in chapter one hundred and four, a theme supported by both the narrative and the structure.

"Earlier we mentioned the Melville revival began with Weaver's biography in 1921. But there were other scholars during the decade—for example, Van Doren, Lawrence, and Mumford—whose works provided fresh insight into Melville's writings and gave impetus to his overall resurgence. But this begs a question: what prompted any of these serious literary critics to write book-length analyses of this all-but-forgotten writer? Well, they started probing the latter half of *Moby-Dick* and diving into those ostensibly discursive chapters full of 'fat,' which Sandra here has counterintuitively now renamed 'muscle.' And what did they discover buried in these digressions, these supposed throw-away chapters? The whale's DNA—seemingly minor characters and their personal stories acting as philosophical rebar informing and strengthening Melville's quest for certitude in an indifferent, cruel, unforgiving world.

"Now I want y'all to put yourselves in these scholars' shoes. Choose a secondary character and explain how that character's story reinforces the overarching theme of the novel. Just to clarify, I'd put Ishmael, Moby-Dick, Ahab, Queequeg, and

Starbuck off limits for this exercise, which still leaves you with, ah, no pun intended, a boatload of characters from which to choose. So who would like to take a shot at 'striking through the mask'? Anyone? A minor character reinforcing a mighty theme."

Bones's hand towered above a sea of bowed heads muttering, "Oh, God, there she goes again."

"Sandra, it looks like you'll be assuming the roles of Van Doren, Mumford, and Lawrence today. So which secondary figure would you choose to illustrate our point?"

"Perth, sir."

During a brief moment of shocked silence following her response, I could hear the inquisitive rustling of notebooks and thumbing of pages. The professor smiled incredulously and asked for confirmation. "Perth? Perth, the blacksmith? Well, after twenty-five years, Sandra, that's a first. We're all intrigued. So why not start by giving us the character's personal profile and then explaining how this tertiary, or perhaps in this case, quaternary figure helps underpin our 'mighty theme.' It's a tall order. Go for it!"

Following the professor's lead, Sandra opened with the profile. "As you said, sir, Perth is the blacksmith on the *Pequod*. Before boarding the whaler, his life has been spiraling downward for years. Melville says, 'He had been an artisan of famed excellence, and with plenty to do; owned a house and garden; embraced a youthful, daughter-like, loving wife, and three blithe, ruddy children; every Sunday went to a cheerful-looking church, [and] planted in a grove.' But one night Perth takes to drink, and 'upon the opening of that fatal cork, forth flew the fiend, and shriveled up his home, his work and his life.' Melville continues, 'The bellows fell; the forge choked up with cinders; the house was sold; the mother dived down into the long churchyard grass; her children twice followed her thither; and the houseless, familyless old man staggered off a vagabond in crape; his every woe unreverenced; his grey head a scorn to flaxen curls!' But 'having left in him some interior compunctions against suicide,' Perth signs on to the *Pequod* and goes awhaling.

"After arriving in the South Pacific, Ahab approaches Perth as he hammers away at a glowing pike head positioned on an anvil—'the red mass sending off the sparks in thick hovering flights, some of which flew close to Ahab.' The old captain asks the blacksmith, 'Are these thy Mother Carey's chickens, Perth? They are always flying in thy wake; birds of good omen, too, but not to all;—look here, they burn; but thou—thou liv'st among them without a scorch.'"

Professor Morton interrupted. "Let's stop here to clarify. Sandra, can you help us with the Mother Carey reference?"

"Yes, sir. She's a mythical figure who, for sailors, personifies the cruelty of the sea."

The professor nodded and asked, "So what are these Mother Carey's chickens then?"

Bones immediately responded, "They're storm petrels, which for sailors represent the souls of dead seamen. Ahab's comparing the flying sparks to seabirds and the souls of sailors."

Professor Morton smiled. "Good research there, Sandra. Please go on."

"Yes, sir. So when Ahab observes the red-hot steel flying about Perth without burning him, the blacksmith explains, 'Because I am scorched all over, Captain Ahab…. I am past scorching; not easily can'st thou scorch a scar.'"

"What do you think Perth meant by that?" the professor asked.

Again without hesitation, Bones replied, "The blacksmith had suffered unspeakable cruelty. He believed the gods had already done as much as they could to him. They couldn't inflict any more pain. And even old Ahab was awed by the blacksmith's courage to carry on. He asked Perth, 'How can'st thou endure without being mad?' In fact, I believe Melville's asking the same of us. How can we persist in light of all the suffering?"

"Well done, Sandra." The professor paused to check his watch and then said, "Looks like we're out of time for today. So next time, we'll wade into *Gravity's Rainbow*. There's a lot to chew on in Pynchon. So come prepared!"

As we walked home from class, I looked over at Bones and said, "Good job today. Do you think anyone picked up on the message you were telegraphing about our suffering?"

"Probably not. It's our problem, not theirs…. Curious, Casey J., if there had been more time, which character would you have chosen?"

I hesitated and then replied, "Let's see… Ah, probably Pip, you know, the slave child."

100

"The boy that falls overboard and is finally rescued?"

I nodded. "Yeah, the boy who sees 'God's foot upon the treadle of the loom' while floating in the ocean; and then after his rescue he goes about the ship half-mad saying, 'I look. You look. He looks.…'"

"Why Pip? What message would you have been sending with him?"

I turned toward Bones, smiled, and said, "That I, you, and everyone like us—we're all seeking certainty in an indifferent, cruel, unforgiving world. That each and every day, I look, you look, and they look in the midst of what Melville calls the 'heartless immensity' of 'awful lonesomeness.'"

"So my suffering and your loneliness?"

"Yeah, pretty much sums up our lives, don't you think, Bones?"

She nodded. "Yeah, sure does, Casey J."

8

THANKS TO STATS WE Outcasts shone brightly in Pantheon's computer science constellation. While Zulu, Bones, and I continued honing our legacy gaming skills playing *Déjà vu*, *Through the Looking Glass*, and *Airborne*, Stats took a part-time programming job in the university computer lab and spent much of his free time studying an array of high-level program languages and visiting Internet relay chat sites to absorb as much technical information as possible.

As in high school, Stats ensured we Outcasts stayed one step ahead of everyone else. While our intro class was learning the Scheme programming language, we were plowing new ground with induction and recursive programs, asymptotic notations, propositional and predicate logic, and discrete probability. By the time the class reached our discrete structure module, we had already moved on to programming in a Unix environment using basic shell commands in the C language.

Some weekends we wouldn't see Stats even though he was right there in the house with us. He would stumble out of his room just in time to shower before heading off to classes Monday morning. When we finally nailed him down, he gave us intriguing glimpses into what was really going on behind his bedroom door. I opened the conversation at dinner.

"Hey, man, it's getting to be a habit—you checking into your room Friday evenings and emerging Monday mornings bleary-eyed, disheveled, and unshaven. Shooting straight with you, Stats, we miss you a lot during the competitions." I smiled and then pitched the pivotal question: "So what ya got going on in there all weekend behind the green door?"

"Solving problems," he replied.

"Personal or programming?" Bones asked.

"Both," Stats said.

Zulu jumped in. "Both? I don't get it, Stats."

"Oh, you know, I'll be writing code for one of the university's databases and invariably hit a brick wall. After staring at the screen for an hour or so, I back off, determined to let the problem simmer for a while, practice a little discipline. But during my walk home from the lab, a solution usually pops into my head, forcing me into my room to pick up where I'd left off."

"But two days straight of programming and ordering in Chinese food?" Bones asked.

"I dunno. I'm fascinated with the challenges. Pushing the limits of what the computer will do. It's damn addictive. You don't want to stop. And honestly, most of the time you just can't stop. I've learned there's nothing more exhilarating than solving for x. You know what I mean?"

We all nodded, and Zulu picked up the thread. "Yeah, we all know it's a great feeling when you sail through the fog and reach shore. But what happens when you get stranded out in the open sea? When you're all alone in rough waters. Must be unsettling. What do you do then?"

Stats smiled. "But that's the beauty of it, Zu. I'm never alone. The boat's full of sailors willing to help me weather the storm."

I probed lightheartedly, "So you're sneaking your shipmates in through the bedroom window, huh?"

Stats laughed and played along. "Not through the window, Casey J. Through the screen—the computer screen. Hanging out with my brothers in the IRCs."

"IRCs?" Bones probed.

"Internet relay chat channels. Text-based forums where you can meet people with similar interests and exchange information real time. Like a chat room, only cooler."

"Information about what?" Zulu asked.

"Almost anything. Sports, statistics, gaming. Sometimes I'll just hang out, relaxing and soaking up the ins and outs of a computer language I'm learning. Other times I'll pose specific programming questions when I hit the wall at work. And within minutes someone comes to the rescue with an ingenious solution. As I said, the boat's full of sailors willing to spring into action. And once they get to know you, they're as caring as family. It's strange. When I'm all alone up there with everybody, it feels comfortable. It really feels like home."

I glanced across the table at Zulu and Bones and said only half-jokingly, "I don't know about you guys, but I get the feeling we've been replaced or are in the process of."

Stats interrupted, "No! Not in your or my lifetime! We Outcasts have shared too much. They're good virtual friends.

But y'all are flesh-and-blood family. And believe me, that's never going to change."

Zulu jumped in, moving us beyond a sensitive subject. "These IRCs as you call them, they sound pretty interesting. Can you show us how we can access them?"

"Sure, Zu. No problem," Stats said. "I think you'll really like it. IRCs are old-school—command lines, hashes, forward slashes. So let's head upstairs, log on to your computer, and see how it's done. Real easy… not rocket science."

After Zulu booted up, she relinquished her chair, and Stats went to work keying and explaining. "In order to talk to IRC servers, you first have to install IRC client software on your computer. Next, you choose a network of servers. There are thousands of IRC networks. Some of the largest are EFnet, IRCnet, Freenode, and on and on. But for tonight's demo, let's head over to Freenode. Now we'll register our 'nick' and password." He looked back over his shoulder at us and emphasized, "Remember, it's a nick, not a handle. So what do you want for your nick, Zu?"

"Warrior1," she replied.

"Okay. Warrior1 it is. Now lean in here and key in a password."

Zulu quickly complied.

"There. Now that you're registered, we're good to go. Let's look at the list of channels and select one." Stats looked back over his shoulder again and said, "Remember, it's a channel, not a chat room." He then pulled up the long list covering every topic under the sun and began scrolling down the page.

He stopped at the channel #python and joined the discussion already under way. While waiting for an appropriate moment to jump in, he explained why he had entered the #python channel. "Python is a high-level programming language. I'm writing some code in it over at the lab. I've got an issue that's been bugging me. Python keeps rounding my floats."

"Whoa!" Bones interrupted. "What's a float?"

"Basically a decimal number. When you place a decimal before a programming statement, you're casting the variable as a float. So let's give it a shot and see what our fellow sailors have to say."

After typing his question into the command line, Stats hit return and his request for help appeared on the screen:

> *[00:13]<warrior1>is there a way to get python to stop rounding my floats? :P*

And within a minute, help was on its way:

> *[00:14]<tyler2>umm what makes you think it's rounding them?*

Stats typed his response:

> *[00:14]<warrior1>well I'm trying to do the BBP algorithm in Python, and it magically stops at 3.14159265359*

From there a back and forth ensued:

> *[00:15]<tyler2>where the same thing in perl,*
> *goes to 3.14159265358979*
> *[00:15]<tyler2>i'm assuming since it's a 9 on*
> *the end, that it rounded*
> *[00:15]<elixir> use print repr(your_pi)*
> *[00:16]<tyler2>ooo?*
> *[00:16]<elixir>str rounds floats to 12 digits*
> *[00:16]<warrior1>I wasn't aware of that*
> *[00:16]<warrior1>thanks man*

Stats looked back over his shoulder once more, smiled, and said, "See, that didn't take long! What do you guys think?"

We all nodded and mumbled, "Awesome, Stats. Awesome."

9

WITHIN DAYS OF THE demo, the irrefutable law of unintended consequences had kicked into high gear. Instead of coaxing Stats out of his room to resume our daily competitions, by showing us what had kept him locked inside his room he had drawn us newbies into his seductive, addictive World Wide Web. As soon as we returned home from classes, the four of us would grab a bite to eat and then scatter to the four corners of the house only to resurface the following morning at daybreak. But while Zulu, Bones, and I were in hot pursuit of every legacy gaming channel on the net, Stats had moved on to a higher level of play, a far riskier form of competition than any of us had ever engaged in before.

About two o'clock in the morning several weekends later, there was a soft knock at my bedroom door. Nothing unusual about one or more of us being awake at that hour. After all, at our tender age, who wouldn't be up as Friday night rolled into Saturday morning? What was unusual was the knock itself. We had all become so consumed by our Internet endeavors, we rarely, if ever, left our rooms to visit one another. Late weekend nights were now all about gaining expertise that could be translated into an advantage when competing at our legacy games.

"Yeah. Who is it?" I asked.

"Stats," the voice whispered. "May I come in?"

"Enter!" I said without taking my eyes off the screen.

"You got a minute? I've got something I want to show you."

I sighed, looked back over my shoulder, and said, "This better be good. We've got a decent thread going here on *Déjà vu*."

"Seriously. I think you'll find it interesting. I sure did."

I logged out of my computer and followed Stats back to his room. He pointed toward the bed. "Take a seat there while I work a little magic." Several minutes passed as he keyed in various commands in starts and stops.

"I know that look on your face, Stats. What are you up to this time?"

"You'll see. Just hold your horses a sec." While he tapped away at the keyboard my mind considered the possibilities. It turned out to be nothing I would have ever guessed. "There!" he said. "Come here and take a look."

"What am I looking at? Looks like some kind of a chart."

"It is. You ever wonder what Professor Morton makes a year? Dean Perkins? How about the Pantheon president? The provost? They're all here."

"My God, Stats, how did you get that?"

"HR."

"Sure, HR just handed it over. 'Thought you might be interested, Stats.' Is that it?"

"Not exactly."

"Well, then, how'd you get your hands on this?"

"Our adviser, Ms. Gardiner."

"She gave it to you?"

He smiled. "Not exactly."

"So fess up. How'd you get it?"

"Ms. G. was getting booted out of several university systems. She asked me to take a look at it for her. She just happened to keep her password to the HR system sitting close to her keyboard. As I began running some diagnostic tests, the index card kept screaming, 'Read me! Read me! I'm easy to remember: f-a-r-m-e-r. For Ms. Gardiner.' When I got back here after helping her out, I could still hear the screaming in my ear. 'F-a-r-m-e-r for Ms. Gardiner.' So I accessed the university network, input her password, and presto! The compensation database was right there for the picking. And that, Your Honor, is the case for the defense."

"If you're not careful, Stats, you're going to need one."

"What's that?"

"A good defense. This is flat-out illegal. And all because your curiosity compelled you to confirm what we pretty much already knew, that they're all making six-figure salaries with a hell of a lot of perks on the side."

"My curiosity? Not exactly."

"Not exactly? Well, clue me in then. What did drive you to do this?"

"Competition."

"Competition? What the… ?"

"Bragging rights," he added.

"Bragging rights?"

"Yeah, bragging rights on one of the channels. It's a game to see who has got the biggest balls. Nobody's changing anything in the databases, just sniffing around. Pretty exciting to go online and announce to the world you've accessed the compensation system at Pantheon University."

I shook my head. "Man, oh man."

"If you've got the password and you're not messing around with the data, the risk's infinitesimal. But the reward of earning some online at-a-boys is priceless." Seeing what must have been a horrified look on my face, he added, "For God's sake, it's just a game, Casey J. Like the *Oregon Trail, Airborne,* or *Through the Looking Glass.* No difference except for the adrenaline rush and the pounding heartbeat as you move around through the system. I'm telling you straight. It's flat-out fun!"

I shook my head again and started for the door. I stopped midstride, turned around, and said, "Just remember, Stats, if you get caught, your ass is grass and you're on your own. You hear?"

"Yeah, I hear you loud and clear; but nothing's gonna happen, Casey J. You'll see."

My talk with Stats did nothing to coax him out of his adrenaline rushes. Instead, he came up with a new scheme to take the adventure to the next level. He convinced the lot of us to take part-time jobs, not to earn extra money, but to "help the Outcast team raise its level of play in global competition!"

Somehow, we didn't take much convincing. But while Zulu, Bones, and I were busy garnering worldwide kudos for collecting passwords and gaining access to patients' records at a retail chain pharmacy, consumption data at the local gas company, and money market accounts at the savings and loan, Stats had raised the stakes even higher.

There was another late-night knock at the door.

"Speak!" I said.

"It's me," Stats whispered. "May I come in?"

"Yeah."

"You have a minute? I've gotta show you something."

"We'll have to make it quick, Stats. I've got to get to bed. Early out in the morning to open the branch."

"Sure. No problem. I'll make it quick."

I followed him back to his room and took a seat on the side of the bed. He began keying, and within minutes the credit card accounts of a regional retailer appeared on the screen.

"Another notch in the belt, Stats?"

He smiled and nodded. "Yeah."

"How'd you get the password?"

"This one's special, Casey J. That's why I had you come over here."

"What's special about it?"

"I didn't have the password."

"So how'd you pull this off?"

"Hacked in."

"Hacked the system? How'd you learn to do that?"

"Lurking in restricted forums on the deep web. It's all still pretty new to me… but I'm learning."

"What the hell's the deep web?"

"The digital underground. The ninety-five percent of the Internet hidden away from standard search engines. You need to download special software, Tor, to access the sites. This software protects your identity through encryption and bouncing your packets to a number of relays run by volunteers around the world. Tor keeps snoopers from learning the sites you visit and keeps the sites themselves from discovering your physical location. Here, let me show you how it works."

Stats keyed in a lengthy, nonsensical ".onion" domain name and off we went into the lower depths. It was as if we had turned off of a brightly lit Main Street and onto backstreets lined with brothels, pawnshops, flophouses, and greasy spoons. The cast of characters included pushers, pimps, hitmen, and thieves.

"So Tor gets you to an online black market, huh?"

"Well, yes and no. Think of it more as a marketplace. Something like the Chor Bazaar in South Mumbai, where you can buy the legitimate and the, ah, questionable. It's not all contraband. You have lawful trade in, for example, clothes… books… paintings."

"So what do you have under 'Jewelry' there? Click on it. Let's see."

Stats hesitated before clicking on the link.

"Well, what do we have here? 'Uncut stones. Gold. Silver. Other precious metals.' And all obtained on the up and up for sure. What's hiding beneath that 'Money' link there?"

Stats sighed and clicked on the link.

"Let's see. Looks like the sellers are a bit more forthright. We have stolen credit cards and travelers' checks, and we have counterfeit bills in 'discreet denominations in most popular currencies.' And do we need to check the 'Pharmaceutical' link?"

But before I could suggest skipping it, Stats stoically clicked on the link.

"My God, Stats, there are hundreds of drugs for sale here. All legal too, I'm sure. And conveniently alphabetized within categories: cannabis, Ecstasy, psychedelics, opioids, stimulants. And what's this? 'The Arsenal.'"

Stats stared at the screen and clicked on the link.

"It looks like we'll be all set, if we ever have to go to war. We have Berettas, Glocks, SIGs, Smith & Wessons, AR-15s, AK-47s. And what do we have at our disposal under 'Services'?"

Stats looked back over his shoulder and smiled guiltily as he clicked on the link.

"Aha. We've hit the gusher! 'Hacking'! So click on the subheading here. My God, how many hacking sites are there? Must be at least twenty of them!"

He spun around in his chair and glared. "After I peel the sarcasm off the back of my head, Casey J., I want to get serious for a minute."

"Serious? As if this isn't serious enough? What is it?"

"If Zulu, Bones, and you decide to try out the deep web, remember, stay away from anything labeled 'chans,' 'bulletin boards,' or 'CP.' Friends on the web have warned me it's really perverted, illegal shit. Stay away from it."

"Enough said, Stats. But tell me. You learned how to hack the retailer's system on these sites?"

"Yeah, a couple of them. But they're small potatoes. The big boys host forums in Russia and its satellite states. Those sites weren't very useful, though. They're all conducted in Russian."

"Maybe that's a good thing."

"Why's that?" he asked.

"Keeps you from getting arrested and sent up the river."

Stats laughed.

But my admonition did nothing to turn the tide. Instead, by the end of the week Stats had managed to convince me and the two women in the house to order four sets of interactive language software for Russian—levels one through five.

10

ONE NIGHT AS WE were closing in on the Thanksgiving holiday, I heard a soft knock at my bedroom door. "Не сейчас, Stats!" I said. A pause and then another knock, this one more insistent than the first. "Уходи, Stats!" I shouted. And then still another knock. "Боже!" I screamed as I slammed my mouse down and raced to the door. I growled in our embargoed language, "This better be import—" but stopped midsentence when I saw a stranger standing in the hallway. Well, she wasn't exactly a stranger. Her name was Erin and she sat next to me in Professor Morton's lecture hall. She had asked earlier if we could meet to discuss our next assignment, Richard Powers.

"Erin! I'm sorry. I thought it was Kevin, one of my roomies."

"If this is a bad time, Jason…"

"Oh no. I was just, ah…"

"May I come in?"

"Sure, no problem. It's a little cramped in here with all the stuff. But you have a choice—the leather chair or the side of the bed. Take your pick."

"The chair's fine. Thanks." She smiled nervously and said, "Forgive me for asking, but your shouts and the signs in Cyrillic taped to everything downstairs—the chairs, the tables, the cabinets…"

"Oh, that's Brenda's doing. Another of my roomies. She's also the author of the 'English-Free Zone' notice posted on the front door. No mystery here. We're all studying Russian this semester and are trying the total-immersion approach. But she's even more gung-ho than the rest of us, since she's taking Russian history to boot."

"I suspect it was Brenda who answered the door and started asking me unintelligible questions in what I now know is Russian. I got the vibe she doesn't like taking prisoners."

"Tall, thin, long brown hair?"

"Yeah, that's her." Erin shook her head.

I laughed and said, "It's one of the reasons we call her Zulu. She's a warrior, a driven soul, and mixing a metaphor, I'd agree there's not a lot of veneer on the tabletop. But believe me, you want her on your side. She's a team player. Fearless. A blind dog in the butcher shop. Would tear down the gates of hell to help you out."

Erin smiled and after an awkward silence changed direction. "As I was saying after class last week, I wanted to talk to you about the Powers assignment because you had a lot of insight into Pynchon. To be honest, I was a third of the way through *Gravity's Rainbow* and was about to give up. The disjointed narrative, the hundreds of characters, all the historic and scientific allusions, the puns, the technical jargon. My God! But then during our class discussion, you suggested the dedication—the dedication to Fariña—as a good way to pick the lock."

I smiled, not because of what she was saying but because of how her words made me feel. It was the rare act of someone saying something both positive and, more importantly, genuine about what I had done or said. I jumped in before embarrassment could overtake my euphoria. "I have to admit, though, Erin, I had an advantage over most of you in the class."

"How's that?"

"My father grew up a folkie. On a trip back East years ago he saw Mimi in concert north of Hartford at some nature center, I believe. That was some years after the accident that killed Fariña, after she had picked up the pieces without really ever moving on. You can't imagine how often my father told that story about the concert and all the details surrounding Richard and Mimi's time together. Married in April '63 with his college friend, Pynchon, as best man. Buried almost three years to the day after the wedding, with Pynchon now serving as pallbearer. He had watched his friend, Fariña, scream across the sky and die randomly west of Cachagua, die just as the Londoners who'd watched the V2s arc and rain down randomly."

"A random indifference."

"Yes," I said.

"And paranoia the cure, which defines us."

"Yes, indeed."

"The devil in the mirror."

"'God's foot on the treadle of the loom,'" I replied. "'If man will strike, strike through the mask!'" she shouted.

I smiled and whispered, "'I look, you look, he looks; we look, ye look, they look.'"

"And the end of truth seekers?" she asked.

"Reduced to dreams," I said.

"On telepathic flashes?"

"On omens, and all pointing to terror."

"And ambiguity."

"And absurdity."

Just as our verbal pas de deux ended, the music stopped. "You mind if I flip the side?" I asked.

Erin shook her head and said, "Vinyl, huh?"

I nodded. "Yeah."

She pulled out an MP3 player and said, "Just got tired of the hassle, cleaning the stylus and disks, keeping the albums out of the sun and away from heat. Now I just download everything and take my music with me wherever I go."

"Yeah, convenience is the MP3's strong suit, but I like the richness of the vinyl analog. The grooves mirror the original waveform. No information's lost there or when the output's fed directly to the amp. The waves are more accurate. Fuller. Adds richness to the overall sound."

"Daft Punk you're playing?"

I smiled, "Close, but no cigar. Kraftwerk, the godfathers of electronic pop. Düsseldorf. The 1970s. My roomie, Kevin, likes to say, 'No Kraftwerk, no everything after Kraftwerk.' These guys were a couple of decades before Daft Punk. You could think of the bands as separated by time but connected by sound, synthesizer, and style."

"What's the song?"

"The title cut of their '74 album, *Autobahn*. The bass riff frames the music. I suspect it's a synthesizer bass patched into a sequencer. I'm telling you, in the realm of electronic music these guys were pioneers and are now gods."

"But I've heard people say electronica's for nerds."

"They're as thick as shit!" I blurted. "Sorry, Erin. They just don't have a clue how much hip-hop and dance owe to Kraftwerk. Especially here in the States. No Kraftwerk, no hip-hop. Simple as that."

Erin glanced toward the music and pointed to a photograph above my bookshelf stereo. "You're really into ships, aren't you? Let's see, there are six pictures on the wall and…"

"And eight scale models scattered about," I said. "Even some packets of coal on the nightstand there, perhaps from the starboard bunker in the aft corner of Boiler Room No. 6, where Fireman Dilley testified the fire broke out."

"All pictures and models of the same boat?"

"Yeah, a very famous one. The RMS *Titanic*."

"How'd you become interested in that?"

"It was when I saw *part* of the DiCaprio-Winslet movie on cable—before my mom made me turn it off. She thought the film was a 'little too advanced'—translate that 'too risqué'—for me, since I was only nine years old. You know, the nude scene where Jack sketches Rose posing naked, wearing Cal's engagement necklace. But Mom in her inimitable way resolved her angst by renting me another movie about the sinking, *A Night to Remember*. It's regarded as the most accurate ever produced. I watched it in awe that first time, and from then on I was hooked."

"But what really intrigued you about the *Titanic*? The sinking?"

"It wasn't so much about the ship as the fascinating cast of characters on board the night she sank. Second Mate Lightoller ordering twenty-five men out of lifeboat 2 at gunpoint so women and children would survive. 'Get out of there, you damned cowards! I'd like to see every one of you overboard!' Thomas Andrews, the naval architect, who witnessed the *Titanic*'s fleeting arc from birth to death, standing alone in the first-class smoking lounge as the boat slipped beneath the sea, gazing at Wilkinson's painting, 'Plymouth Harbor,' arms folded across his chest, a lifejacket nearby. And then there was Wallace Hartley, a violinist, leading an eight-member band in waltzes, dance tunes, and hymns, calming passengers as they piled into the lifeboats, soothing them almost to the end. But unlike Andrews's fate, Hartley's body was recovered weeks later, the press reporting he was 'fully dressed with his music case strapped to his body' à la Ishmael, the *Pequod,* and Queequeg's coffin."

"I'm impressed. How do you remember all these fine points?"

"Easy. I still play that VHS every year on the anniversary. Let's say, to pay my respects."

Erin nodded and looked away again. She pointed toward the floor-to-ceiling rack of computer equipment occupying the far wall and said, "Looks like photographs and models aren't all you collect. Are they old PCs?"

I shook my head. "No, not exactly. They're Macs."

Sad to say it was her innocent pulling of a third loose thread that caused my studied discipline to completely unravel. I leaned in and continued excitedly, "Early SEs. Quadras. IIs. The first with a mere forty megabytes of hard drive space and four meg of RAM! Think of it!"

"But why?"

"You mean why collect them?"

"Yeah. Why collect a lot of old computers?"

"Partly because of competition with my roomies."

"They have walls of old equipment too?"

I nodded. "Yeah."

She turned away and stared at the wall. "I just don't get it."

"Because you're the other!" I exclaimed.

"The other what?"

"The other on the inside looking out."

Erin shifted in her chair, glanced down at her phone, and said, "My God, it's already past six o'clock. I wish I had more time, Jason, but I have to get back to the dorm before they stop serving dinner at seven."

"You could stay here and have supper."

She stood up and began buttoning her coat. "Ah, I wouldn't want to put you out. Besides, I promised, ah, a friend I'd meet her at the dorm for dinner tonight."

"But what about Powers?"

"Oh. We'll have to reschedule. I mean, if that's okay with you."

"Sure, sure. No problem."

Erin opened the door and looked back. "Thanks for the invite, Jason."

I nodded and began moving toward the door to escort her downstairs. She raised her hand and said, "No worries. You get back to your work. I'll show myself out." She smiled and then pulled the door shut behind her.

I stood motionless at the center of the room for some time, arms folded across my chest, staring at my favorite picture, the last known photograph of the *White Star* giant snapped as she slowed at Red Bay, Northern Ireland, to drop off a local pilot who had guided her out from Queenstown. I turned away; carefully placed a new vinyl on the stereo; moved over to the side of the bed; turned off the light; and buried my head in my hands.

In my mind's eye I could see Erin still sitting there in the leather chair staring at the wall of computers. "I just don't get it," she said.

"Because you're the other!" I exclaimed.

"The other what?"

"The other on the inside looking out. You see, Zulu, Stats, Bones, and I—we're the polar opposites. We're the outcasts on the margins looking in. No offense but y'all put us out there too. And it's always been like that. Teachers, counselors, classmates, principals—all of you speaking freely amongst yourselves within your circles. But God forbid if we encroached on your space. The mood changed. Y'all would speak and act so differently. The teachers, counselors, and principals adopting a cool, distant air of guarded professionalism. You students bullying us or treating us as jokes. Weirdos. Fools. And after a day of desperately trying to fit in, we'd retreat to our bedrooms, curl up under the covers, and try separating ourselves from the pain.

"You're still staring at the equipment stacked on the wall. You're shaking your head. What do you see? Old boxes? Outdated tools? Recyclable metals and plastics? You know what we see, Erin? We see old, reliable friends who never betrayed us, who were there for us like family in the darkest days. Unlike you folks, we put a premium on loyalty. We would never cast off the few predictable, rational friends we've ever had.

"The music now? Kraftwerk again. *Tour de France Soundtracks* honoring the one hundredth. No, Erin, it's not about what we hear but what we suffer as we listen. We feel the relentless climb from the Gap to Alpe d'Huez. One hundred seventeen miles of grueling switchbacks finishing in the thinnest air, digging deep into our reserves. Legs burning. Lungs burning. Repeating the mantra on the climb, 'Keep driving; conquer the gradient; vanquish the pain.' For what? For a pride only we can feel. Fifteen stages down now with five to go. But in truth we delivered the verdict today without grand celebration. Time to retire now and prepare for the next stage. Rest easy tonight, heroes. The Grand Depart trophy was won today. The glory will come in due course and follow us all the way to the grave."

11

ERIN KEPT HER BACK to me, bantering with a classmate until Professor Morton entered the room. As she opened her notebook, she said, "Good to see you, Jason."

I looked straight ahead and whispered coolly, "Likewise, Erin."

The professor stepped away from the lectern, waved his hands to quiet the class, and opened his performance with an outside-the-box notion. "I've decided to take a professional risk," he announced. He paused, moved his arm from side to side in a sweeping motion, and added, "Because y'all will be teaching Powers today."

The room murmured uneasily.

"So who's the brave soul who'll venture a start?"

Bodies slumped and heads drooped as the students avoided eye contact at all cost.

"Well, let's go at it this way then. Anyone who hasn't finished *The Gold Bug Variations*, please excuse yourself now." He paused and scanned the room. "No one? Okay, then. So the working assumption going forward is everyone here has read the novel and is well qualified to impart some insight to the rest of us. Let the games begin. So again, who will get us started. David?"

"Ah… ah…"

The professor turned to another student and pointed. "Sarah?"

"Well, ah…"

He paused and stared up toward our row. "Erin?"

"The ah… ah…"

Bones fired her hand into the air.

"Here we go again," Professor Morton muttered before recognizing her. "Okay, Sandra, can you help us get started?"

"Yes, sir."

"Well then, come on down to the lectern here and impart some knowledge to the rest of us." As Bones approached, Professor Morton asked, "So, Sandra, where would you begin?"

She turned around toward the class, grasped the lectern with both hands, leaned in, and responded confidently, "I'd start at the Vatican, 1509."

The professor, who had moved from center stage to the wings, said, "The Vatican? Interesting. Continue."

"From there I'd move westward to the Royal Alcázar of Madrid, 1656."

Professor Morton nodded. "Intriguing. Go on."

"And from there I'd circle back to medieval Paris, 1163."

"I suppose you're going to connect all the dots for us, correct?"

"Yes, sir."

The student body en masse groaned and rolled its eyes. Undeterred, Bones carried on. "So starting with the early sixteenth century, Pope Julius II commissioned a young Raphael to redecorate the papal apartments. The artist began with the pope's study, which housed the papal library. Since grand venues demand great subjects, Raphael graced the blank walls with massive frescoes emphasizing the close ties between Greek philosophy and Christian doctrine. In one of his masterpieces, *The School of Athens*, Raphael celebrates human achievement by depicting an imaginary forum of the finest mathematical, scientific, and philosophical minds of antiquity. And with this singular fresco Raphael rescues these spurned geniuses from Dante's medieval limbo, thus providing posterity a window on Renaissance thought that 'man is the measure of all things.'"

The professor eased in to help connect the dots in Bones's argument. "On to the Royal Alcázar of Madrid a century and a half later?"

"Yes, sir. King Philip IV of Spain commissioned an aging court artist, Diego Velázquez, to paint a family portrait, which would hang in one of the large halls of the Alcázar, the royal palace in Madrid. Again, since grand venues demand great artistry, Velázquez created a complex, revolutionary work hovering midway between classical and modern art and operating on two levels—the real and the illusory.

"On the surface, the painting, *Las Meninas*, or *The Maids of Honor*, appears to be a straightforward rendering of some of the key figures in King Philip IV's court. You have the young princess, Margaret Theresa, surrounded by her entourage, including her bodyguard, her chaperone, two handmaidens, two dwarfs, and a dog. The artist includes himself in the picture. He's standing at a large canvas immediately behind and to the right of the princess and her entourage, staring out beyond the frame toward the viewer and painting a composition positioned well outside the pictorial space.

"But the plot thickens. First, what's the subject of the work Velázquez depicts himself painting? And second, if this is a 'commissioned portrait of the royal family,' where are King Philip IV and his queen, Mariana? The answers to both questions are captured in a mirror hanging on the far wall behind the princess, her entourage, and the painter. The mirror reflects the heads and torsos of the king and queen. But is the image a likeness of them standing outside the pictorial space alongside the viewer, or is it a reflection of the canvas Velázquez is currently painting? What's the reality here?"

Bones paused, and the professor jumped in. "And now you'll be taking us back to medieval Paris. To the twelfth century, I believe?"

Bones nodded. "Yes, sir. So church architecture for a thousand years had been characterized by thick walls, massive support pillars, and small, rounded arch windows. These early interiors appeared cavelike—gloomy, cold, and cramped. But in 1163 a visionary laid the cornerstone on a revolutionary approach to the architectural skeleton. He employed a rib-vaulted ceiling and flying buttresses, which supported the upper part of the walls bearing the highest compression load. The new ceiling and buttresses allowed for thinner walls, fewer support pillars, and massive windows punctuating the exterior. It was a true triumph of the intangible where sweeping spaces, soaring stained-glass windows, and celestial light joined to create a heaven on earth.

"And since this grand gothic statement in stone and glass presented new acoustic challenges, sacred composers pushed their singers in new directions as the cathedral rose around them. In the span of a mere century, Léonin, Pérotin, and other anonymous members of the Notre Dame School transformed simple, single-line plainsong into complex, four-part polyphony, which would later foster the likes of Palestrina, Beethoven, and Bach. As one contemporary church leader proclaimed, 'The Notre Dame School gave us our first taste of developed harmony transporting our souls into the society of angels.'

"So we see then great venues demand mighty themes, and I might add here, vice versa. Melville surely agrees. Earlier in the semester we read a passage from *Moby-Dick*: 'No great and enduring volume can ever be written on the flea, though many there be who have tried it.' We see the tendency in Melville. We observe it again in Pynchon. And now we see it in Powers. All three constructing imposing structures to support their grand themes."

Professor Morton interrupted again. "If I'm reading you correctly, Sandra, you plan on discussing Powers's use of structure to support and inform his major themes. Correct?"

"Yes, sir, exactly."

I looked over at my fellow Outcast, smiled, and thought, "What else would Bones be discussing? She's playing on her home court dissecting the *Bug*'s skeleton!"

"So where do we begin?" the professor asked. "First, by calibrating the genre. I believe we can stipulate we're dealing with literary fiction that's not dramatic comedy or tragedy, epic or short story. So by process of elimination we conclude *The Gold Bug Variations*, just as *Moby-Dick* and *Gravity's Rainbow* before it, is a novel of the first order."

Professor Morton eased in again. "Yes, and meeting the criteria Professor Watt laid out in his pioneering work, *The Rise of the Novel*—individualized characters, detailed descriptions of setting and situation, 'interpenetration of plot, character and emergent moral theme.'"

"Yes, sir. And then the question becomes, 'What kind of novel are we dealing with when we consider Melville, Pynchon, and Powers?' That question demands further calibration. I'd call *Moby-Dick*, *Gravity's Rainbow*, and *The Gold Bug Variations* 'encyclopedic novels'—voluminous, complex books weaving the arts, sciences, history, philosophy, theology, and cultural milieux into the narrative."

Professor Morton's excitement overtook him as he interrupted again. "So you've read Mendelson's landmark essays, 'Gravity's Encyclopedia' and 'Encyclopedic Narrative'?"

Bones glanced down, embarrassed. "Sorry, sir, but I'm not familiar with the essays."

Professor Morton shook his head and mumbled to himself, "Unbelievably perceptive. Out of the mouths of babes." He nodded toward Bones and said, "Please go on."

"Like medieval encyclopedists, Melville, Pynchon, and Powers discover, retrieve, and arrange blocks of preexisting narratives and knowledge to help build the frameworks for their cathedrals."

The professor once again couldn't contain his enthusiasm. "If not Watt, then surely you've read Clark?"

"No, sir."

"Eco and Frye?"

"No, sir."

"So these are all your own thoughts?"

"Yes, sir."

He shook his head and played devil's advocate, adopting a playfully sarcastic tone. "But really how creative is that, Sandra? I mean writers appropriating other folks' material rather than creating it themselves."

"But they're like great poets juxtaposing words and phrases and fusing them seamlessly into the line. A creative spark arcs the phrases, adding significance and meaning. So you have a power to the third—what the poet creates, what she borrows, and what the reader brings to the work from his or her own experience. And in this regard Melville, Pynchon, and Powers are also syntactical architects, fashioning these blocks of new and preexisting narrative and knowledge into sentences and then paragraphs to, so to speak, buttress the thematic compression load."

Professor Morton threw his hands into the air and responded lightheartedly, "Game, set, match to Sandra!" He paused until the laughter died down then asked Bones, "Did you ever read T. S. Eliot?"

"Yes, sir. In high school. 'Prufrock' and, ah, 'The Waste Land.'"

"*The Sacred Wood*?"

"No, sir."

"It's a book of his early literary criticism. In one of his essays on the Jacobean playwright Philip Massinger, Eliot writes, 'One of the surest of tests is the way in which a poet borrows. Immature poets imitate; mature poets steal; bad poets deface what they take, and good poets make it into something better, or at least something different. The good poet welds his theft into a whole of feeling, which is unique, utterly different from that from which it was torn; the bad poet throws it into something which has no cohesion.'" The professor paused and smiled, "So if Eliot's on board with the approach, then I guess we'll have to get on board too."

He looked out over the host of literature majors and said almost as an aside, "By the way, for you upper-level students continuing on with your grad work here at Pantheon, we offer a workshop focusing on postmodernists. For example, next spring's graduate seminar will be 'More Is More': Gaddis's *Recognitions*, DeLillo's *Underworld*, and Wallace's *Infinite Jest*. But I digress. Sandra, please continue. Tell us about Powers's use of structure to support and enrich his themes in *The Gold Bug*."

As the professor spoke those words, I thought, "Oh my God, from a foul shot to a layup. First she was talking about skeletons and now she's moving on to DNA!"

Bones enthusiastically picked up the thread. "Well, sir, the novel's structure mirrors a central focus of the work: the quest to unlock the secrets of DNA. For example, as there are four base pairs comprising the various 'rungs' of the double helix, there are four main characters here—Stuart Ressler, Jeannette Koss, Franklin Todd, and Jan O'Deigh—whose two love stories, separated in time by twenty-five years, intertwine to form a 'double helix' of attraction, love, and loss.

"And just as genetic experiments have shown that it takes three bases to encode an amino acid for protein production, Powers interweaves three major story lines encompassing three different time periods: 1957–58, when Ressler makes scientific discoveries while listening to Bach; 1983–84, when O'Deigh, Todd, and Ressler become friends; and 1985–86, when Ressler has died, Todd is off doing his own investigation, and O'Deigh leaves her librarian's post to spend a forlorn year alone studying molecular biology and Bach, trying to reconcile herself to the loss of a friend and a lover.

"And speaking of Bach, Powers's title, *The Gold Bug Variations*, hints that Bach's *Goldberg Variations* will play a significant role in Powers's novel. And as we later learn, they indeed do both from a thematic and a structural perspective."

"Stick to the *Variations*' influence on structure for now, Sandy," Professor Morton interrupted. "We'll get to theme a little later on."

"Yes, sir. So Powers divides *The Gold Bug* into thirty chapters plus an introductory section called 'Aria' and a closing one called 'Aria Da Capo e Fine,' which tracks to the architecture of Bach's work consisting of an aria, thirty variations, and a final summary of the initial aria. In addition, Powers uses Bach's keyboard masterpiece to emphasize and legitimatize the encyclopedic nature of his own work. And it was no accident he chose the *Goldberg Variations* from some eleven hundred works in the BWV catalog. Powers understood the *Goldberg Variations* explore a variety of genres and styles in a large number of keys and time signatures and sum the sweep of Baroque musical composition from 1600 to 1750, when Bach died."

Professor Morton raised his hand and said, "Good job, Sandy. We'll have to leave it there. So moving on now from structure to the major themes in *The Gold Bug Variations*, who would like to begin?"

After several false starts by upperclassmen confusing symbol and motif for theme, I raised my hand, and the professor called on me I suspect mostly out of desperation. "So, Jason, can you help us get out of these blind alleys and onto the interstate? Sandy's built us a beautiful Mercedes. We've all piled in. But we're having trouble finding someone who can drive the Benz."

I nodded. "I'll try, sir."

"Go for it then!"

"Yes, sir. Sure on that shining night humans first peered out into the firmament and sensed awe, we became seekers. On a grand scale the most subscribed religions share one thing in common, adherents seek a more perfect state: Hindus looking to reverse the diversity of creation and return to the ideal Oneness; Jews aiming to uphold their obligations under the covenant they'd made with their Creator-God; Muslims seeking complete submission and obedience to Allah; Christians striving for eternal life; and Buddhists yearning to escape a world of human suffering.

"Melville, Pynchon, and Powers tap into this primal theme in their masterworks where personal 'seeking' within the narrative acts as potent metaphor for human questing on a philosophical level. While Ahab seeks revenge and the *Pequod*'s outcasts crave brotherhood, Melville strikes through the mask exploring the mysteries of the 'heartless voids and immensities of the universe.' While Slothrop and several colleagues seek to uncover the secret of the Schwarzgerät, which was to be mounted in a special V2 rocket with an unusual serial number, 11/00000, Pynchon wants 'to break out—to leave this cycle of infection and death.' He says through a character, 'I want to be taken in love: so taken that you and I, and death, and life, will be gathered inseparable, into the radiance of what we would become.'"

I paused to let the beauty of Pynchon's lines resonate before continuing. "Which brings us now to Powers and *The Gold Bug Variations*. At the narrative level Ressler joins a team at the University of Illinois in 1957 seeking to decipher the genetic code. Twenty-five years later Jan O'Deigh, a reference librarian, and Franklin Todd, Ressler's coworker in a data-processing center, join forces in an attempt to unlock the mysteries of Ressler's past. Why did he leave his post when on the cusp of discovery? Why did he disappear only to be discovered years later working as the night supervisor in a Brooklyn computer lab?

"In the meantime, at the philosophical level, Powers explores the yin and yang of human isolation and the unbearable fragility of belonging. After falling in love with a married team member, Jeanette Koss, Ressler develops an innovative approach to cracking the genetic code inspired by a recording of Bach's *Goldberg Variations*, which Koss had given him earlier as a present. For some time Ressler lives with the mistaken impression Koss will leave her husband for him. But on the brink of a scientific breakthrough, Ressler learns she will stay with her husband and abandon the team. He too leaves the project and drops off the grid for decades.

"While investigating the mystery of Ressler's past, Jan O'Deigh and Franklin Todd follow a similar path. O'Deigh falls in love with Todd and leaves her lover. But over time the two drift apart, leaving them to live separate lives of isolation and despair."

The professor moved over to the lectern and asked, "Do you have anything else to add, Jason?"

"No, Dr. Morton," I replied.

He scanned the lecture hall and asked, "Does anyone here have a different take on Powers?"

The upperclassmen shook their heads and mumbled, "No, sir."

The professor turned and addressed me directly. "Good work, Jason, I was on board until you threw the curve at the very end. Doesn't the fact that O'Deigh and Todd reconcile after Ressler's death challenge your argument that Powers's theme is about isolation and the fragility of relationships?"

I replied respectfully, "I don't think so, sir." I opened the novel to the last page and read Todd and O'Deigh's words:

He [Todd] made a great show of collating, a little courtship dance of paper-shuffling to win me again, for good. 'Come on. Let's do it. Let's make a baby.'

I shook my head. 'No,' I said, dead sober. 'It wouldn't be enough. A man like you will always want the real thing someday. Or at least the chance. It would never last.'

'My dear Ms. Reference.' He edged over to me, taking me up against him. 'Why do you think the Good Lord invented sperm bank donations?... And let me ask you another thing. One for the perpetual Question Board.... Who said anything about lasting?'

I closed the book and then concluded politely, "I believe Powers and his characters see an eclipse lurking just below the horizon."

12

STRICTLY ADHERING TO THE spirit and letter of Zulu's law, Stats requested a "substantive" meeting on the front porch just outside the English-free zone. After everyone had taken his or her customary seat on the swing or the front steps, Stats virtually gaveled the meeting to order and said, "Now that I've become somewhat proficient at least at reading Russian, I've weaseled my way into several of the major hacking sites. Wasn't easy, that's for damn sure. Just hanging around for hours on end at some of the channels building trust. And by the way, that's the good news."

"And the bad news?" I asked.

"I'm so far behind these guys they can't even see me in the rearview mirror. It's another world over there. All custom shit. They'd kick me into kingdom come if they knew I had been script kiddieing."

"Script kiddieing? I thought we were speaking English here," Zulu said.

"That's what you call a newbie building off another hacker's programs rather than writing his own code. But so far so good. They've allowed me to lurk without challenging me. But if they ever do, they'll ferret me out in a heartbeat and ban me from all the hacker sites for good. Word gets around fast about minor leaguers. So I just keep my head down, keep quiet, keep soaking up as much as I can.

"But I got to thinking, if we're ever going to get significantly better as a team, I'm going to have to really get serious about this. Spend a lot more time writing code and trying to hack into really secure networks."

"Geez, Stats," Zulu said. "Hack into more networks? You're just increasing the risk that one of these sites, be it government, business, or otherwise, is going to nail your ass."

"And ours too!" Bones added.

Stats shook his head and smiled. "Do you really think I'd raise the risk exponentially and take the chance of getting y'all in serious trouble? Do you think I want to drive us into the ground? I'd take a hit too. After all, I'm piloting the plane. So how about this for starters. What if we devised a plan where I could write custom code and then try hacking into a network where I had the owners' permission?"

"Who in God's name is gonna do that?" I asked. "What would be in it for them?"

Stats laughed aloud and responded, "The thrill of matching wits. My offense against their defense."

"Okay, Stats, so whose playing defense here?" I asked, as if the sense of foreboding I felt hadn't already foretold his response.

"You, of course, Casey J. My offense against your defense on a network I'll set up for you."

I stood up and began pacing. "How in the hell would I match wits with you, Stats? I'd get creamed. What kind of competition is that? You'd be winning every match in minutes."

"It'll be my job to see that that doesn't happen."

"You're gonna let me win some of the time to make it look good?" I asked snidely.

"Hell no!" he shot back. "What good would that do either of us? If the objective is to step up my game, then your game has to improve too."

"And how do you propose pulling that off, a lobotomy?"

"Come on, get serious, Casey J. I'll set up an in-house network here with the server running a Linux-based OS. We'll upload a number of popular programs and configure the system without any security beyond the default settings you need to get her up and running. I see this situation all the time when I'm out lurking about. For starters, we'll replicate a national retail operation and work our way up the chain to the toughies, later simulating perhaps a tech company, a wireless carrier, maybe even a government agency or two. You know, simulating their environments, adding the bells and whistles as we go along, like a specialized application firewall and professionally developed network security software, to make it tougher."

"I still don't get it, Stats," I said. "How am I supposed to get up to speed first trying to protect the network against your attacks and then learning how to patch the bugs and vulnerabilities once you've exploited them? That will take a lifetime."

Stats nodded. "So it'll take time for you to assimilate all the ins and outs. No problem. That's where I come in. During the initial and intermediate stages, I'll do the hacking based on the latest I've learned from the deep web. And then we'll work together to strengthen network security and at the same time lengthen your wheelbase. And once you're really up to speed and we're evenly matched, it'll be dog eat dog. I'll attack remotely from the university computer lab at any hour of the day, and you'll be the system's administrator, running your own simulated IT department defending the network here anyway you can. It'll be hand-to-hand combat day in and day out. What do you say?"

As Stats made his case, I began warming to the idea for a host of reasons. I loved the challenge of a daunting task. Stats had a way of getting my competitive juices flowing. And the thought of his offense matching wits with my defense fit our mind-sets perfectly. He was constantly incorporating sports imagery into his conversations, and the phrases were always about the offense attacking to reach a goal. He wanted to "power the baseball up the middle," "run the pigskin downhill," and "drive the lane hard and draw the foul." I, on the other hand, was all about defense. But could it have been any other way, having grown up watching replays of legendary counter-punchers with my dad? The Will of the Wisp, Sweet Pea, Lights Out, the Galveston Giant, and Sugar Ray making them miss and then making them pay.

Stats stood up, extended his hand, and asked, "You in?"

I nodded. "All in."

"Remember, Casey J., it's not the triumph but the struggle. Not to conquer but to fight well."

I stroked my chin and joked, "Hmm, now where have I heard that one before?" I paused and then responded to his paraphrase with a direct quote, "Citius! Altius! Fortius!"

He laughed and said, "Touché, Baron! Touché!"

It was hard to swallow; but early on in the game, every day was a bad day at black rock. As expected, it wasn't a question of *if* but *when* Stats would crack the Outcast server. Struggling to keep my head in the game, I shifted the paradigm for measuring success from the number of wins and losses to how long I could keep Stats, as he would say, "out of the end zone." But I have to give him credit; he remained committed to the cause, spending hours on end demonstrating how he had penetrated the network and then explaining how I could strengthen the system and make it less vulnerable to attack. The learning curve was beyond steep—firewalls, ports, SQL injections, cross-site scripting, trivial file transfer protocols, Netcats, and on and on. Sad to say, despite his coaching, every time I stuck my thumb in the dam, plugging a leak, another appeared almost immediately.

And I wasn't the only one feeling the pain. Poor Bones and Zulu, who were predisposed to rooting for underdogs, not only had to suffer through my endless string of humiliating defeats but had to listen to my daily rants of frustration, too. While they couldn't suggest any specific technical help, they were nice enough to join me after classes for lunch at the 7.0 and offer up their moral support. We followed the same ritual every other afternoon. After placing our orders, I would lead off venting my growing rage and despair. Zulu and Bones would then follow, first commiserating with me and then providing updates on what was new and exciting in their own lives.

I opened our latest conversation with the usual salvo. "I'm just about to pull my hair out. I know, I know. You keep telling me I'm making progress. Keeping him out of the network for an hour when we started versus keeping him out for up to a day now. But, my God, it's frustrating! I've listened to him. I've studied on my own. I've done everything imaginable to block his attacks—patching the operating system, patching the applications, the browser, and plug-ins, whitelisting applications, installing intrusion and detection prevention, whitelisting web domains and content, installing enhanced workstation firewalls, locking down router access only to ports 80 and 443. What more is there?"

When I realized I was droning on and getting down in the weeds, I paused and shook my head. Bones reached her hand across the table, stroked my arm, and whispered, "I know it's frustrating, Casey J. But keep your eye on the prize. Stats is working hard, and so are you. You'll get there. I promise."

Zulu chimed in with her support. "Bones is right, Casey J. You've never failed before, and you won't this time either. Just know we Outcasts are here to help you any way we can."

I smiled and thought, "If only you could."

After an awkward silence, I followed protocol and asked Bones, "So what's new with you?"

"Nothing much. Been going through the motions in biology this past week. That is, until today. The teaching assistant is walking us through DNA 101—you know, the helix, base pairs, protein synthesis, emphasis on mutations and genetic disorders. Been there and done that. Boring!"

I leaned in and asked, "You said 'until today.' What did you mean?"

"While the TA was lecturing, I drifted back into Ressler's quest to crack the DNA code. You know, drawing insights from Bach's 'Variations.' Remember what Powers said?"

I shook my head. "Keep going."

"Powers suggests, 'The Goldbergs are layered all the way from bottom to top and back down again, with every layer of ordering… contributing to, particularizing, and lost in the next rung of the hierarchy it generates.'"

"I'm confused, Bones. What are you driving at?" Zulu asked.

"What if there's a second genome lurking below the first? The top layer of code expressing proteins as deciphered in the sixties, a second layer controlling genes."

"With all the advances in technology, don't you think we would have found that second layer by now?" I asked.

"You have to think of it as one language being written over the top of another, keeping it out of sight. If the code can transcribe two kinds of messages, any mutations in the protein sequencing may cause disease by altering gene control instructions."

"I'll give you credit, Bones. It's creative. But it's really way out there."

"Well, a half century later we're still chasing down remedies for a number of genetic disorders. A second layer of instruction controlling gene switching provides an elegant solution. I'm just saying.…"

I smiled and responded, "I've got to hand it to you, Bones. You've got a lot of Ressler in you, and that ain't half bad." I paused, glanced over at the third stage of the protocol, and asked, "So what's up with you, Zu? Anything interesting?"

"Yeah. Y'all know I was really bummed when I couldn't find an African history course and had to settle for Russian history. But now that I've drilled down into it, it's really been pretty interesting."

"What are you into now?" Bones asked.

"Well, the Russians call it the Patriotic War of 1812."

"Napoleon's invasion?" I asked.

"Yeah. Fascinating story. General Kutuzov's outnumbered Russian forces fought the French to a draw at Borodino, inflicting heavy casualties before retreating to the far side of Moscow."

"Sacrificing the city to keep his army intact to fight another day?" I said.

"Exactly. Kutuzov restocked his munitions while waiting for Napoleon's momentum to slow. And when the French advance finally stalled, Kutuzov counterattacked and aggressively chased Bonaparte back to the gates of Paris."

Sometimes we are lucky enough to catch a glimpse of a composer at the piano, a painter at the canvas, a programmer at the keyboard, or a writer at the desk. We observe the struggle and mistakenly conclude the artist is "in the moment," that is, he or she is in the very process of creating a new work. But counterintuitively, that instant, the one that truly sparked the imagination, may have occurred hours, days, or even months before in a relaxed twilight where reality can rub up against dreams, freeing the mind to soar.

In fact, what we are witnessing is a visible genome meticulously transcribing thought from memory to a hard drive, canvas, or page—translating a notion into words, notes, numbers, or strokes. In truth, the epiphany will always remain hidden to us because a second, overwritten genome works imperceptibly to tease out the essence of our being. Sadly, we are left only to observe the sculptor tirelessly chipping away to free an earlier vision from the stone.

And so it was with solving Stats's riddle. After settling up at the 7.0, Bones, Zulu, and I returned to the Outcast Headquarters where we headed off to our separate rooms— they to fathom calculus and I to push the network fog well into the night. When I finally collapsed across my bed, I began to dream. I was whipping up omelets, adding two parts Russian history to one part each of genomics and Ali-Forman fight. And while suspended in that metamorphic crucible of imagination, the network solution appeared out of the mist. If I were to ever successfully fend off Stats's daily exploits, I would have to turn the network's conventional architecture upside down and inside out.

13

As Professor Morton entered the lecture hall, I leaned over toward Bones and asked, "Do you think he's finally flipped his wig?"

"I don't know," she replied, "but the touring cap, stereo, and sunglasses are endearing, don't you think?"

I shook my head and shrugged.

Surprisingly, the usually demanding professor ignored our bemused chatter and focused solely on setting up his portable MP3 docking station. When he had finished the setup, he waved his arms and shouted, "Silence, everyone! Silence!" And once he had everyone's attention, he scanned the room, smiled deviously, and added, "Fasten your seat belts. You're in for a helluva ride!"

The professor flipped the switch on the stereo. A brief silence. Then several bars of distorted guitar before the growl began:

In and above men.
In and above men.

Tight percussion and bass slammed into the melody, driving it to double time just before the growl returned:

The fury of waters
Revolving still,
Your voices are silences
When they speak through me.
To the crossroads
We are turning our backs
And in each of your wounds
I will plant a seed of belief

In and above men.

When this first track ended, the professor immediately fast-forwarded to a second equally up tempo tour de force. But the style shifted from aggressive death metal to a more traditional melodic heavy metal sound with a unique blend of Nordic darkness and uncharacteristic sensitivity. The guttural had given way to a deep, clean baritone:

Starts as a feeling pure,
This vitreous second sight
Without hallucinating, hating,
Captive of a future bright

Fortune telling—
Honours for madmen only!

Through the looking glass,
And when the glass looks back.

Why is everything to be denied?
That could make life a little bright.

At the conclusion of the brief concert, the professor moved over to the lectern and asked, "Anyone know the group?"

The tattoos to my left raised his hand and shouted, "Tiamat!"

The professor shook his head and replied, "Right church, wrong pew, Charlie." He scanned the room and asked, "Anyone else want to hazard a guess?"

The tattoos took a second stab. "Katatonia!"

"Another good shot, but the band's not Swedish.... Anyone else?"

Silence.

"Okay, then. It's the Portuguese heavy metal band Moonspell."

The tattoos groaned and asked, "Early Moonspell? I came on board with *The Great Silver Eye*."

Professor Morton nodded and replied, "Yes, 2003." He scanned the class again and probed, "So now that we have the band, the country, and the year, anyone want to venture a guess about the album title? Anyone?... No?" He smiled and asked lightheartedly, "So with a show of hands now, how many of you think I've gone off the deep end?"

The lecture hall erupted with laughter as every hand shot into the air.

The professor continued the banter with a melodramatic flair. He raised his hands to his mouth, twisted the ends of an imaginary moustache, and said in a faux villainous tone, "All you doubters out there, you'll see. There's method to my madness!"

He paused, removed the sunglasses and touring cap, and resurrected his deep, professorial tone. "You'll recall while laying the framework for our analysis of *The Gold Bug Variations*, we discussed the symbiotic relationship between the artists and the spaces inspiring and informing their work. First, there was Raphael, the papal library, and his fresco, *The School of Athens*. Next, there was Velasquez, the Royal Alcázar of Madrid, and the oil on canvas, *Las Meninas*. And then there were Léonin and Pérotin, the Notre Dame Cathedral, and their innovative compositions transforming simple, single-line plainsong into complex, four-part polyphony, giving us our first taste of developed harmony. We concluded then that great venues demand mighty works and vice versa.

"Only months after the Portuguese Revolution in '74, Fernando Ribeiro and José Luís Peixoto were born into freedom nine days apart. As young men they became admirers of each other's work—Ribeiro reading Peixoto's poetry and the poet in turn enjoying the vocalist's hard metal lyrics. The two finally met at a poetry reading and decided to undertake a joint project. It wouldn't be a crossover cliché with Peixoto writing lyrics or Ribeiro crafting songs based on Peixoto's earlier work. It would have to be something new, something innovative. So Peixoto began crafting short pieces based on three of the band's songs destined for their next album. The band reciprocated, composing additional songs inspired by Peixoto's first three short works. And as they say, the rest is history.

"Peixoto's novella, *Antidote*, which you read as part of your assignment for class today, was one-half of the project's output. The Moonspell album we sampled just now comprised the other half. The novella and the album, which share chapter and song titles and overarching theme, were released together on compact disc as a single innovative concept work. And thinking back now to Raphael, Valasquez, Léonin, and Pérotin, we can easily argue that the Moonspell album provided a provocative 'space' informing and inspiring Peixoto's work.

"So with that background in mind, let's now turn to the novella and analyze Peixoto's style and theme. What's the first thing that comes to mind about the style?"

Professor Morton's unorthodox introduction, a Trojan horse if you will, had undoubtedly penetrated the barricades. At least twenty hands were raised, pleading for attention. The professor pointed toward the rear of the hall and said, "Okay, David, how would you describe the style here?"

"It's prose that reads like poetry. I caught myself slowing and beginning to read entire pages aloud. The people in the cafeteria thought I was nuts. The people in the library just thought I was an asshole and threatened to throw me out."

A nodding of heads with knowing laughter.

"Would you mind sharing a passage?"

"No, sir." And after briefly thumbing through the pages, David said, "This is from the seventh chapter, 'Moonlit.'"

He then began reading rhythmically in a cadence reminiscent of Yeats:

> The gleam on the stones of the sidewalk.
> Points of light flickering on the watery film
> left there by the night, by the rain. I walk on
> the sidewalk's pattern of stones, on a carpet of
> illuminated points that flicker and then go out.
> Their life is short. My life is short. Points of
> light that open up paths for me to follow. My
> boots fall amid these points that light up, live
> for an instant, and die forever.

"Good choice, David. Thank you. And it's not really surprising Peixoto would adopt poetic rhythms and imagery for his fiction. Like many Portuguese novelists, Peixoto is also a poet steeped in a long tradition of Portuguese poets, from Camões to Pessoa. In addition, he has written a number of lyrics for fado, the mournful Portuguese songs about longing and loss."

Professor Morton paused to consult his notes and then asked, "How does Peixoto alert us to important themes in *Antidote*?"

A host of hands shot into the air again.

The professor pointed to the lithe redhead sitting directly in front of me. "Okay, Kathy. How does he alert us?"

"Through a careful choice of words charged with multiple layers of meaning as you would find in poetry."

Professor Morton nodded. "Yes, in this case I would agree. Diction is important to understanding the thrust of *Antidote*. But a word of caution here. In the other two Peixoto works you read for today, *You Died on Me* and *The Piano Cemetery*, I don't believe diction would be as reliable an indicator. You have any ideas why, Kathy?"

She shook her head and slumped in her chair.

"Can anyone help us out here?"

Bones pulled the trigger.

"Okay, Sandra, what's your take? Why might diction work in *Antidote* but not so much in the other two works?"

"Because it's not the author's diction in the other two works. They're translations. *Antidote* is not."

"But why is that relevant?"

"While reading *The Gold Bug Variations*, we touched briefly on gene expression. We said it requires two steps—transcription, where the cell makes a copy of the DNA, and translation, where ribosomes use that transcript to synthesize proteins. While *Antidote* is in a sense a transcription, *You Died on Me* and *The Piano Cemetery* are translations. *Antidote* is an exact copy of Peixoto's thinking, whereas the other two works are not. They may contain errors or mutations caused either by the translator or the nuance of meaning within the languages. That's not to say translations are necessarily bad. They are just different because of the intervening variables. And as a result of these differences, translations may be inferior to, on par with, or in some rare instances, superior to the original."

"Very good, Sandra. So if Peixoto's diction is not always the best indicator alerting us to important themes, what stylistic device might be more reliable here?"

A fresh bed of reeds now swayed in the wind.

"Let's see.... Peter, can you help us with another stylistic device?"

"How about repetition. Words, phrases, sometimes whole sentences."

"Exactly. You have a favorite example for us, Peter?"

"Yes, sir." He stammered while trying to find the passage. "In *Antidote*, in the chapter 'A Walk on the Darkside,' the young woman enters a garden of memories to recall cherished times she'd shared there with her lover. Peixoto uses repetition to emphasize her sense of separation and loss. She reminisces:

> I'm sitting on the edge of the bench where we sat in dreams.... My gaze slowly passes over this bench. I see you. I don't know if this face is you or the image of you in my memory. I see you. I don't know if I see you.... Wherever we look, in us or outside us, nothing but darkness. I stop seeing you as I stop seeing the earth, the trees and the garden.... I remain. Perfectly still. In silence. I don't know whether the face, the gaze, the gleam I saw was you or was the image of you in my memory.... Perfectly still. In silence.... If I wanted, I could say your

name. But I don't know if you're here. I remain.
Perfectly still. In silence.

"Thanks, Peter. So while Raphael created a greater sense
of depth and shadow in *The School of Athens* by scraping into
the plaster and increasing the amount of carbon or bone black
pigment in his mixtures, Peixoto, the word painter, uses both
diction and, most reliably, repetition to add philosophical or
intellectual heft to significant passages."

The professor paused to consult his notes before speaking
again. "Let's spend our remaining time talking about important
themes in Peixoto's work and how they relate to earlier themes
from Melville, Pynchon, and Powers. Who would like to offer
up a theme, one that runs through Peixoto's work and the major
works of our previous writers. Who would like to begin?"

An embarrassment of hands continued.

"Okay, Sarah, how about getting us started."

"Well, we said earlier in the semester the themes 'seeking'
and 'human isolation' inform the major works of Melville,
Pynchon, and Powers. We have a number of isolated seekers—
for example, Ahab and Perth in *Moby-Dick*, the villainous
Blicero in *Gravity's Rainbow*, and the four characters in *The
Gold Bug Variations*. Peixoto explores similar themes in *You
Died on Me*, *Antidote*, and *The Piano Cemetery*."

The professor interrupted to make a suggestion. "The
three Peixoto works we read were written over a six-year
period from around 2000 to 2006. So, Sarah, why don't you
start with the earliest work, *You Died on Me*, and we'll work

up chronologically from there. Tell us, who is separated from whom in *You Died on Me*?"

She picked up her copy of the brief work, marked a passage with her index finger, and explained, "The narrator has returned to his boyhood home in the south of Portugal. He looks out the back window toward the garden and trees his father had planted years before and recalls his father's life and early passing. The narrator reminisces:

> The night falls slowly. I said I would never forget. And I remember. The night fell slowly, and at this hour at this time of year you unrolled the hose with all the precepts and following certain rules you watered the trees and the flowers in the yard. And you taught me all of that.… You left so much of yourself behind superimposed on the indifferent bitterness of this world that pretends to carry on. Your movements. The eclipse of your gestures. And all of this now is too little to contain you. Now, you are the river and the waterfront and the spring. You're the day, and the afternoon inside the day, and the sun inside the afternoon. You're the whole world because you are its skin. Dad.

"In essence, and paradoxically, the narrator seeks and discovers a pathway to reunion through memories of his father."

"Excellent, Sarah. Someone else now. Who wants to tackle *Antidote*?"

 Another sea of hands.

"Mark, you want to give it a shot?"

"Yes, sir. A young man and woman meet in the street, fall in love, but end their lives separated from each other and isolated from family and friends."

"What drove the couple apart?" the professor probed.

"Fear," the student replied.

"That's right. In fact, the first chapter, 'In and Above Men,' opens with a personification of fear acting as a Greek chorus: 'We flow like blood inside bodies whenever they're pulled down and swallowed by chasms.... Inside and above people, we are fear.... We know that you know us.... At some time in your life we filled you and wrapped you with the image of our voice, the image of our meaning, silence and words. At any time we choose we can fill you and cover you again.' So, Mark, what frightens the young couple enough to drive a wedge between them, isolating them from everything and everybody?"

"The young woman had a birth defect, a deformed chest, which embarrassed her. Since childhood, she had worn her blouse buttoned up to the neck."

"And the young man?"

"In the fifth chapter, 'Antidote,' Peixoto writes: 'The first time the boy felt fear was when his mother explained that his father wasn't coming home. On that day he realized that there are things that go away and don't come back.' The young man never forgot that feeling of loss and avoided relationships where he could experience that awful pain again."

"So one more thing, Mark, before I let you off the hook. In the same paragraph, Peixoto writes: 'Their fear was a poison.' Since this particular chapter and the overall work are both called 'Antidote,' what do you believe is the remedy for their fear? Is it committing suicide as the young man does here? Or is it just giving up and dying as the young woman does? After all, characters in earlier Peixoto works—for example, José, the shepherd, in *The Implacable Order of Things*—choose a similar path. José uses a rope and a live oak to end his suffering, which is a 'continuation of suffering.' So is death the antidote to our fate. To our painful existence?"

The senior literature major didn't hesitate. He flipped through the novella and read the last sentences of that same paragraph: "'Among the words uttered by the mother and the teacher, they'—the boy and girl—'could discern the word courage. And they could feel thirst on their lips. Fear, poison. Courage.' I don't want to jump the gun here, but the Ishiguro quotation at the beginning of *The Piano Cemetery*… I believe it captures what's really in Peixoto's heart. Ishiguro writes, 'There is nothing for it but to try and see through our missions to the end, as best we can, for until we do so, we will be permitted no calm.'"

Trying to hide his appreciation of Mark's interpretation, the professor flashed only a glimmer of a smile before playing devil's advocate. "But how do you explain the suicides and the early deaths in Peixoto's prior works?"

The senior squarely planted his feet and confidently returned serve. "I just don't believe his earlier characters had caught up to his thinking—to endure with grace and grow stronger through the suffering."

After a pause to allow the message to resonate, Professor Morton looked over at the student and said, "Solid, Mark. Real solid. And the Ishiguro quote is a nice segue into *The Piano Cemetery*. So what separates us, isolates us, here?"

Again, many are called, but few chosen.

"Okay, Jason, we haven't heard from you today. So what separates the characters in *The Piano Cemetery*?"

"Death. But picking up on Mark's comments, Peixoto's not arguing for early death, suicide, or just giving up. The marathoner, his father, and his grandfather set the example by seeing the missions through until the end. Peixoto emphasizes that it's through death we paradoxically live on. A part of us survives in our sons and daughters. The marathoner's father dies just as his grandson, Hermes, is born. The marathoner dies just as his son, Francisco, is born. The name, Francisco Lázaro, as well as the torch, have been passed on to the next generation."

"And the name, Jason. What about the name? Besides being the actual given and surname of the Portuguese marathoner who died in the 1912 Olympics, do you see any other relevance?"

"I suspect it's the Portuguese equivalent of Lazarus, whom Jesus raised from the dead. So the name reinforces the resurrection theme. The name and the DNA are passed down from parent to child."

The professor eased in almost with a whisper:

Would it have been worthwhile,

To have bitten off the matter with a smile,

To have squeezed the universe into a ball

To roll it towards some overwhelming question,

To say: 'I am Lazarus, come from the dead,

Come back to tell you all, I shall tell you all'—

He paused, glanced at his watch, and moved to the side of the lectern. He scanned the lecture hall, then cleared his throat and said, "Since this is our last class together before the final exam, I want to leave you with a few closing thoughts." And just at that moment, the Baroque Master tripped a substation breaker. The lights flickered, dimmed, and faded to black.

The professor moved over into the smoky chiaroscuro between the bone black void and the bridled white slanting in through the narrow casements. Arms outstretched and feet hovering just above the stage floor he became a marionette or perhaps a crucified saint. He resumed his benediction: "Your insight about space inspiring and informing the artist's work compels a closer look now at the *Cemetery*. An earlier view, just a physical space piled high with castaways, a site for youthful fantasies and domestic cruelties. But also metaphor for the poet's stash of memories from which to draw while burnishing a phrase or rounding a thought.

"But now I see there's more. Much more. The Lázaros are cabinet makers who would rather be crafting pianos. But the cruel reality of the purse steps in. And at the opposite end of the earth years later, a towheaded boy stares into the looking glass and conjures up the next Keats. The light gleams an instant, then it's night once more. The bearded boy peers in and now sees Serebryakov mouthing Shaw's maxim, 'He who can't, teaches.' So alas, poor Yorick. Consigned to the church-yard till a month past doomsday. The air is now full of his cries. A charnel house! A charnel house! He can't go on. He must go on! Must see the missions through to the end.

"And then your insight, your indomitable, infinite space. A closer reading and slowly, brightness fills the piano cemetery. O death, where is thy sting now? O grave, where is thy victory?"

The professor paused, pointed out into the lecture hall, and waved his arms slowly from side to side. He whispered, "I can grow old now in this new, mysterious, magical place of dreams and trysting. My old Francisco to your new. My codon to your protein. My penumbra to your first light. A shared journey seeking *your* cemetery now that I've found mine. Remember, no resurrection without the night. I look, you look, we look."

He then peered out over the multitude and declared, "'All the thirsty can now approach.'"

14

THEY LEFT ME HERE alone in the apartment with the echoes, fending for myself and still seeking my own cemetery. The embargo was the first thing to go. After our second semester, Zulu traveled to Saint Petersburg to continue her Russian history studies at the university she proudly claimed was founded by Peter the Great. The other shoe dropped several months later when Bones and Stats announced they were going to try making a go of it as a couple in the Babylon district on the west side of town.

While my fellow Outcasts had been cast to the wind, their ideas about genomes, Napoleon, and professional sports had taken up permanent residence in the software I had been developing to once and for all lock Stats out of the Headquarters system. Yes, Stats may have changed venues, but the long-standing game was still afoot *mano a mano*. And with a potent mixture of deadmau5, Tool, and caffeine a la the 7.0, I made good progress toward building the fortress and setting the trap.

In fact, I was hard at work debugging the software when the telephone rang. It was Stats inviting me to dinner at the 7.0 after classes that evening. Since I hadn't seen him in more than two weeks, I gladly accepted his invitation and explained I would reserve the regular spot and wait for him there.

As he neared the table, fashionably late as usual, he began offering his apologies and excuses. "Sorry, Casey J.! Sorry! Got hung up with Professor Thompson. I just couldn't get away." He skidded to a stop, hoisted his backpack up and off his shoulders, and collapsed into the chair across the table from me.

Before we could launch a conversation, a tall, thin waitress with a long ponytail walked up and said, "Good evening, gentlemen. My name's Lynn. I'll be your compiler tonight. Before we get started, I'd like to query, you're regulars here, right?"

I nodded. "Correct and we'll both be ROMing."

"Copy that," she said as she whipped out her PDA. "So for booting up, what'll it be?"

"The usual. A Handler," I answered.

"Bits and bytes?" she asked.

"Sure, why not?"

"Next?"

"Spaghetti Code."

"Megahertz?"

"Absolutely."

"Anything else?"

"A Bundle."

"How would you like that done? Stock or overclocked?"

"Overclocked," I said.

"Expanded or compressed?"

"Expanded. The bells and whistles."

"Backend application?"

"What do we have today?" I asked.

"Cookies and Drive Surprise."

I smiled. "Okay. I'll bite."

"Floppy or Hard?"

"Floppy."

"To drink?"

"Java straight."

"Mega or gig?"

"Make it a gig."

The waitress turned to Stats and asked, "And for you, sir?"

He just smiled and proudly replied, "I'll make it easy on you. I'll be having what he's having."

"Yes, sir. I'll be right back with your Handlers and drinks."

After she disappeared around the corner, I asked light-heartedly, "So how's married life treating you?"

Stats shook his head and said, "You sure got that right. All the warts are there without the preacher and the paper. It has its ups and downs, Casey J. More downs than ups right now. But to be expected, I guess, during a shakedown cruise. I've known Bones since kindergarten. And I thought I really knew her. But being around someone isn't the same as living with them."

I nodded and kept out of the way.

"She's forever on my case about my knuckle cracking," he said, "but sees nothing wrong with moving through the apartment flapping her hands when she gets upset about something. And the sensory stuff? Forget it! She almost kills me rubbing my back. I'm forever having to tell her to lighten up. She says she's sorry. But heavy pressure's the way she's always

164

liked it. Then she'll want to hold hands. I do my best to hide my disgust. For the life of me, I don't see what people get out of trading clammy palm sweat. And oh my God! Kissing! It's like smashing your face into someone's nose and mouth. Ugh! But the pièce de résistance was when her mothering instincts kicked in. She really put the squeeze on for a dog, and she knows damn well I'm deathly allergic to their dander. It just drives me nuts!"

Sensing he was finally running out of steam, I eased in and asked, "Is there anything that you *do* like?"

He managed a half smile and responded honestly, "I think she's beautiful. I really love her. And you know, I never want to be without her."

"Well, I'd say that trumps all the static. Agree?"

"Yeah, no question about it, Casey J. No question about it."

After the waitress dropped off our java and Handlers, I asked, "Is that why you had me down here for dinner? To talk about the shakedown?"

He smiled broadly and answered, "Of course not. The invitation was extended to inform you your system's been cracked again."

"Shit!"

"Hey, a month ain't bad, Casey J. You've made great progress."

"How'd you hack in this time?"

"You let your guard down. A stupid mistake with a port. Let's drop by the computer lab after dinner. It's easier to show you than trying to explain it to you."

"Just when I think I'm getting somewhere."

"Hey! You are! You really are! That's why I wanted to have dinner. To let you know you're now ready for the last level. Ready for the big time!"

"The big time?" I asked.

"Well, first we'll make sure the system's real solid. Next, I'll try hacking my way in. If I manage to penetrate your defenses, I won't be telling you from now on. I want you to figure it out on your own that your system's been cracked and then I want you to see if you can neuter or kill me."

I managed to hold my composure even though I was busting a gut inside. I shook my head and stammered, "I don't know if I'm ready, Stats. Sounds like a tall order to me." But Stats was too absorbed in his bits and bytes to listen.

We finished our meals, then walked over to the computer lab. It took Stats a mere thirty minutes to explain his latest exploit, review the Headquarters system remotely from top to bottom, and declare the network totally clean and secure. We were primed for the next battle.

In my mind's eye it was Stalingrad, November '42, with two hundred twenty-five sniper kills to my credit. The Germans had ordered their best marksman from Berlin to 'neutralize' me. Their Major König would be the hunter and I the hunted. But patience, camouflage, decoys, and diversions would help me ferret this huntsman out. I would study his methods and

166

movements and patiently wait for that one instant when I could squeeze the trigger, delivering one well-placed shot.

So it was nearly seventy years to the day after the storied sniper duel in the Stalingrad rubble that I confidently loaded Thunderwood 7.0 onto the guard device fronting the old Headquarters network just beyond the DMZ. I chose the name "Thunderwood 7.0" for two reasons: first, because I keyed most of the code either at Headquarters in the Thunderwood district or at our favorite hangout, the 7.0, and second, because the firewall appeared deceptively as soft as pine while having the capability of concealing an unexpected and potentially lethal counterattack below.

It was an innovative approach inspired by Zulu's General Kutuzov, Bones's theoretical second genome, and Stats's Muhammad Ali. Thunderwood 7.0 worked by establishing a parallel network on a virtual machine. Before any of Stats's probes reached the Headquarters network, they first had to pass through Thunderwood 7.0, where his probes were fooled into thinking they were moving about in the real network. Thunderwood 7.0 alerted me that Stats was in the virtual system and allowed me to monitor his movement, tag his address, and then draw a bead on him to deliver that one well-placed shot.

The trick was to create a honeypot, which would allow Stats to penetrate the virtual network without making it too easy and tipping him off that something was up. I decided I would overlook a security patch for a piece of software Zulu had insisted we load onto the system for a project she was doing. As it turned out, she rarely used the software, and none of the rest of us ever did. Don't get me wrong, as the newbie doing hand-to-hand combat with Stats, I religiously kept the software up to date. But it would be plausible to slip up occasionally and overlook an obscure clunker that none of us ever used.

So now the long wait began. I knew he was coming, but I didn't know when. To the right, a charred, hollowed-out tank. To the left, a Nazi pillbox. Had the Major crawled into either? No, no way. The tank's Swiss cheese and the pillbox gun port were sealed shut. But there in the center between the two, a sheet of iron with bricks piled up on it. Why not a foxhole dug beneath the iron sheet with escape trenches added during the night? Let's check it out. I put my glove on a thin stick and raised it. The Major took the bait. He was out there. But where? Let's check the glove. No slant to the bullet hole. Dead on straight. He was there under the metal.

The telephone rang. I knew who was calling. I didn't have to check the software for alerts. Stats was telephoning to declare success while completely avoiding an announcement.

"Hey, Casey J.," Stats said in his upbeat voice. "I haven't spoken to you for a while. Haven't seen you on campus. So what's up?"

"Nothing much," I replied. "What's up with you, Stats?"

"Just calling to get you on board for our party."

"Party? What are we celebrating?"

"Our one-year anniversary. Just think of it. Bones and I have been together for a year now."

"That long, huh?"

"Yeah. Seems like we only moved out yesterday."

"So, Stats, whom should I be nominating for sainthood, Bones or you?"

"I'll be deviously gracious here and recommend Bones for canonization." He paused to segue from banter back to subterfuge. "So can I count on you for the party?"

"When is the fête?"

"A month from tomorrow. It'll be special, too!"

"How's that?" I probed.

"Zulu's coming home from Russia just in time for the celebration. She emailed day before yesterday."

"That's cool. So where are we holding the gala?"

"Where else? Our hangout—the 7.0. So can I count you in?"

"Of course you can. Count me in."

As Stats droned on about this and that and how well everything was going, I returned to Stalingrad and relived one of my two hundred twenty-five kills. I watch a Nazi officer climb confidently out of his bunker and begin ordering his troops around this way and that. As I train my scope on his bare head, I know he doesn't have a clue that he has only a second or two more to live.

I checked the system. Despite his best efforts, Stats had managed to trip multiple alarms while bumping about in the corridors of the virtual network. But it was time for patience. I had to allow Thunderwood 7.0 to do its work—monitor his movement, capture his server address, and copy his password and system ID. I was determined to do just as Stats had instructed me. I would employ extreme patience and check off all the boxes.

Now it was the hunter being hunted. Patience. Just wait. I was in the afternoon shadows. The Major was directly in the light. A flash near the edge of the metal. A shard of glass? A telescopic sight? I raised the crown of myhelmet. The Major fired. I shouted out in pain and then waited. The hunter lifted the sheet. I saw a sliver of his forehead in my lens.

I had everything I needed then—the server address, the open port, Stats's ID and his unique but characteristic password. I smiled. It seemed so obvious then. I asked myself, "What else could his password have been but 216EmOrYsT, the address of Ruth's boyhood home in Baltimore."

I took a deep breath. I slowly squeezed the trigger while aiming intentionally high and to the right, firing a warning shot rather than going for the outright kill. I chose to spare the university network and Stats's reputation, pride, and part-time tenure. Instead of defacing the university system, I changed Stats's password to "Short Line," effectively locking him out of his own network. And once he deciphered the mysterious hack, he would know his fellow Outcast had not only learned to defend but also to counterattack.

15

A FTER STATS AND BONES left our intimate fête of four at the 7.0 to do what I suspect couples do on their anniversaries, Zulu and I had a chance to sip house Zinfandel and talk about her yearlong stint at the university in Saint Petersburg. "So, Zu, before dinner you said you made a midcourse correction shortly after your arrival in Russia, but you never got to finish because the waiter came by to take our orders."

"Yeah, changed majors again."

"Let's see, you started out in African history and then switched to Russian history. So where are we now? Lichtenstein?"

"Cute. But are you ready for this?"

I nodded while pretending to hold my breath.

"Theater!"

"My God, Zu! Theater? You've gotta be kidding me."

"You heard me right. Theater."

"So what happened in Lapland to change your mind all of a sudden?"

"A class I lucked into during my first semester. It was sort of a hybrid course—you know, a mix of history, literature, theater, and music. The course I had planned on taking, Imperial and

Revolutionary Russia: 1700–1917, was totally booked with a waiting list. Then I saw they were offering this course on contemporary culture and politics and jumped in. Since I'd read a lot about the former Soviet Union, I figured it would be fairly easy and give me a chance to get better acclimated to my surroundings before hitting the heavy stuff."

"But out of everything in the course—history, literature, theater, and music—you chose theater? How's that?"

"If I had to sum it up I'd say the new Russian drama just speaks to us."

"Speaks to *us*, Zu? You've gotta help me out here."

Zulu smiled and asked, "You have an hour or two to talk about Kremlin politics and economics?"

"Anything for you, Zu. I hate admitting it, but I really missed you. I thought a lot about the good old days when we went out trick-or-treating, seeing the neighbors' faces when they opened the doors and saw us standing out there, you dressed as Prince Charming and me as Cinderella."

She nodded and smiled. "In an odd way it felt right, Casey J. I had always been a tomboy. Loved playing sports, going hunting, and wearing boots and jeans."

"Yeah, and I confess I love women's fashion—the patterns, the bright colors, the way the materials feel and flow across my skin."

Zulu shook her head. "Yeah, the good old days," she said, "when I could be you and you me."

I laughed. "A scary thought, Zu. But, at the same time, calming. Comforting." I paused to envision the possibilities before circling back to Russian politics and economics. "So, Prince, you've got the floor from now all the way to closing."

She reached across the table, stroked my arm, and whispered, "It feels really good when you know someone cares enough to *want* to listen."

"Yeah, I know, Zu, I know." And after a mutually perceptive pause, I continued in an upbeat tone, "So, Zu, you really do have to help me out here."

"Well, the dissolution of the Soviet Union was a supernova. Everything came unglued in the late eighties: politics, the economy, culture, the society. Gorbachev's gamble, his policy of Glasnost, just simply blew up."

"Glasnost?"

"Yeah. It means 'openness.' Gorbachev theorized that by relaxing government controls, he could overhaul Russian society without undermining the power of the Communist Party. But the policy turned out to be a disaster for the government. Along with freedom of the press came the inevitable discrediting of the state-run newspaper, *Pravda*, and the dispelling of myths sustaining the Soviet system. And then the next thing coming down the pike was Perestroika."

"What's Perestroika?"

"It's a blend of economics where you've got both state ownership and free enterprise. But instead of implementing a coherent policy, the government introduced a series of Band-Aid programs. As they dismantled much of the planned economy, they implemented a private sector that lacked the strong support of a commercial legal system and an updated infrastructure. The bottom line of all of this was the Russian people lost their jobs and identities."

"So no one really knew how to get a free market up and running?"

"That's right. And the chaos overtaking their politics and economics was also being reflected in the theater. You see, theatrical communities were struggling with their own identity crises. Before Glasnost the theater was chained to socialist realism, a policy dating back to the Stalinist period in the thirties calling for the instructive use of literature, art, and music to advance the socialist state. After Glasnost, you were free to try anything and everything. But while many playwrights were eager to write plays tackling the various ills plaguing the country, the dramatists faced resistance from old-style Soviet-educated directors who refused to stage the new works because they frankly didn't know what to do with them. So a temporary fallback position for most directors in the early nineties was to retreat to the past, staging Chekov and the forty-seven-play repertoire of Alexander Ostrovsky to fill out their seasons."

"So plays like *The Cherry Orchard* we read in high school?"

"Ah, I'd say more like *Uncle Vanya* and *Ivanoff*. But be that as it may, the prevailing sentiment was that Russian theater and playwriting were dead or at least in the last throes."

"So you're signing on to the dead and dying, huh? You've gotta help me out some more, Zu."

She smiled knowingly and said, "No problem, Casey J. Granted, while supernovas represent the explosive death of the past and present, they also signify the violent birth of the future. And out of that theatrical chaos a new approach to playwriting was born. It was during Moscow's Lubimovka Playwriting Festival in '97 that the theatrical community got its first taste of the future with Oleg Bogaev's avant-garde production, *The Russian National Postal Service.* Unlike playwrights of the past, Bogaev viciously and directly attacks social issues using absurdist theatrical techniques, which up until Glasnost were just flat-out taboo!"

"What's this Bogaev railing about? The poor quality of the Russian mail service?"

Zulu smiled and responded to my obvious teasing. "It's a helluva lot more than that, Casey J. You have this old fellow, Zhukov, who, forgotten by God, country, family, and friends, is busy celebrating his seventieth birthday while slowly slipping into senility. Zhukov spends most of the play writing letters to himself on the basis of being someone else—cosmonauts, the president of the country, the director of television, and the cockroaches living in his ceiling. Every time he falls asleep, Vladimir Lenin and the queen of England show up, arguing over the role of the Proletariat as well as which one of them will inherit Zhukov's estate after he dies. When Zhukov wakes up, he reads the letters and responds."

"In a sense you have *Krapp's Last Tape.* I mean the loneliness, the separation, especially the separation from self."

Zulu nodded. "Yeah, you're on to something, Casey J. You see, the festival audience split into two camps, with one side declaring the work a train wreck and the other calling it a masterpiece worthy of Ionesco and Beckett. But I think the play goes well beyond the absurd in paving the way for the new Russian drama. I believe Bogaev got a 'threefer,' if you will."

"So beyond the absurd?"

"Well, first there's the social critique, the satiric assertion that like Zhukov the Russian people were losing their identity; and second, there's the theatrical critique. Zhukov's one-man-band post office circulating letters going nowhere fast symbolized the state of Russian theater. Playwrights and directors were in a rut. They were busy trying to come to terms with a Russian past that was highly irrelevant in the new order of things."

"So Bogaev was the be-all and end-all of the New Drama?"

Zulu laughed aloud. "You didn't really think you'd get off that easy, did you?"

I shook my head and answered honestly, "I was just playing with you, Zu. Carry on. It's interesting."

"So after Perestroika blew up, Yeltsin tried what he called 'shock therapy' in '92."

I shrugged my shoulders and asked for clarification. "Shock therapy? I know it's radical but..."

"It's no-holds-barred. You pretty much wipe out any remaining governmental interference in the economy: abolish state subsidies, remove price controls, privatize government-run industries, encourage free trade, and so on."

"Did it work?"

"Yeah, it worked all right. Destroyed the remaining central economy and left people struggling in a corrupt and confusing free-market economy."

"So what did they do to get out of the death spiral?"

"They voted for 'strong leadership' in the likes of Vladimir Putin, who promised to end the economic, social, and political upheavals of the previous decade. But to Putin 'strong leadership' was synonymous with tight control."

"Clamped down hard?"

Zulu nodded. "Yeah, on everything. First, he consolidated power within a few people and agencies. Next, he shut down many free media outlets. And then he fired up the propaganda via government-controlled media, including a majority of newspapers and all the national television stations. If there's a problem, Putin can choose to ignore it or spin the issue any way he wants because the media have no teeth. They aren't going to bite. The remaining journalists in the free press are afraid to raise their heads for fear of expulsion, imprisonment, or even death."

"But has your New Drama tried filling the void left by the neutered politicians and the press?"

"Well said, Casey J. You saw where I was headed. The new breed don't go at Putin or his politics directly. They expose his heavy-handed incompetence by exploring the most significant social issues of the day."

"So who is included in this new breed?"

"Emerging lions like Oleg and Vladimir Presnyakov. Maxim Kurochkin. Yaroslava Pulinovich. Yury Klavdiev. They're all good in their own way, but I prefer Pulinovich and Klavdiev over the others."

"Why's that?"

"It gets back to that 'speaking to us' we were talking about earlier. Identifying with characters we know, with ideas and feelings we sense deeply. That's not knocking Kurochkin or the Presnyakov brothers. They're holding up their end of the bargain addressing mainstream social problems centered around the role of capitalism and the corrosive yearning for the white-washed past. On the other hand, Pulinovich and Klavdiev get at the issues plaguing Russia's youth and the underbelly of Russian society."

"The outcasts, huh?"

"Yeah, that's right. The outcasts creating identity out of chaos."

I smiled and said, "So tell me a little about the works of our sister and brother."

"Pulinovich has two monologues, *I Won* and *Natasha's Dream*, which have gained a following via university productions, laboratory theaters, and most recently at international festivals. The two young women featured in the monologues are reared in very different environments—one in an upper-class household, the other in an orphanage. While Natasha Vernikova enjoys a comfortable middle-class lifestyle, her overly protective mother controls her every move, demanding she follow a rigorous schedule and live up to society's expectations of women. Her mother believes that everyone should have his or her own special trait... that a well-rounded individual is a person who knows how to communicate with others without being just like everyone else. And yet by the end of the piece, Natasha Vernikova realizes that despite having played by her mother's and society's rules, she still lacks an identity. She realizes the persona she projects is a shallow lie.

"The other young woman, Natasha Banina, grows up in an orphanage after her mother is killed by a pimp. During her years there in this hell on earth, she is frequently beaten and mentally abused. Once she escapes the inhumanity, she begins believing she can overcome the stigma society places on orphans—define herself, find her own identity. She dreams of a normal life, the same as other young women enjoy. But this vision of a better life proves illusory. After mistaking a reporter's intentions, Natasha falls madly in love with him. She envisions the reporter helping her transcend her past. But when she learns he is already in a serious relationship, she senses her dream unraveling. So Natasha settles on revenge. She beats the reporter's girlfriend into a coma and is then, ironically, damned to an identity society imposes on her."

"You said the new breed doesn't go at Putin or his politics directly but still manages to explore the most significant social issues of the day. What does that mean?"

"I've warned you the monologues are oblique attacks. So let's tackle the relationship between Natasha Vernikova and her overly protective mother in *I Won*. After suffering through the political coups, financial collapse, and the rise of organized crime, the teens of the turbulent nineties grew up, married, and had children of their own. Since they believe social, political, and economic conditions have improved only slightly under Putin's leadership, they've adopted an understandably conservative approach to parenting.

"They give their children very little freedom and closely supervise their activities outside the home, monitoring their every move, like walking to school, taking public transportation, or spending time at their friends' houses. As graduation nears, they actively steer their sons and daughters toward the university, believing higher education will insulate their children from social, political, and economic change. But while their approach to parenting is well intentioned, it ultimately proves harmful both to their children and to Russian society overall. The children end up echoing their parents' identities, become self-centered, and express little interest in politics or social problems."

"And the Natasha of *Natasha's Dream*?"

"The major thrusts here are the condemnation of the orphanages and the long-term impact the institutions have on the orphans' lives. Pulinovich shines a light on the overcrowding, the abuse by staff, the malnutrition, the horrific living conditions where children remain isolated from the outside world enjoying little individuality, freedom, or privacy. There may be only one toilet per twenty orphans, and it's open for all to see. Children diagnosed with physical impairments—cleft palates, crossed eyes, speech impediments, and the like—are often also classified as mentally deficient and shunted off to 'gulags' of neglect and limited education. The outcome of the current situation under Putin's watch? A steady stream of undereducated adults lacking a sense of self flowing into the underclass of Russian society."

I looked away and whispered, "Oh, ye frozen heavens! Look down here. Ye did beget this luckless child, and have abandoned him."

Zulu gave me a quizzical look and shrugged her shoulders.

"Pip," I responded.

"*Great Expectations*?" she asked.

"No, Melville." I sucked my teeth. "Now what about our brother, Klavdiev?"

"Grew up in Togliatti, some five hundred miles southeast of Moscow, a major industrial manufacturer of automobiles—that is, until the collapse of communism and the economy. Togliatti became a free-fire zone for organized crime and youth gangs. So what would a young Klavdiev do growing up in a city riddled with crime, corruption, and gang wars?"

"Join a gang, I suspect."

"Yes, but you only get half-credit, Casey J. Klavdiev became a gun-toting thug by day and a poet by night. Eventually the playwriting trumped the lawlessness. He left the gangs in '02 and fortunately joined the New Drama movement. I got to see a performance of one of his earliest works, a semiautobiographical one-act monologue, *I Am the Machine Gunner*. It's a brilliant, poetic meditation on the quest for identity in a maelstrom of violence. A street thug comparing his gangsterism to his grandfather's participation in the Second World War."

Zulu reached into her briefcase and retrieved a folder. She thumbed through the pages and said, "Listen to the gangster sitting alone after a firefight, drawing the parallels and reflecting on his grandfather's bravery:

Then I sat down next to the car and…looked at my watch. I was curious—how long had it all lasted? Ninety seconds. Grandpa, grandpa, fuck me. How in the hell did you do that for four years if a minute and a half here was like this?

"This deep appreciation for an older generation answers the Captain from the Presnyakov brothers' dark comedy *Playing Dead*. Klavdiev argues that the youth are not apathetic but are rather in the midst of an identity crisis. Near the end of *The Machine Gunner*, the grandson—and I believe Klavdiev as well—explains the revelation he had while fighting in the gangs:

All that bullshit, all that "take one for the team," and "no surrender" and "we're not giving up Moscow!" That all came to him! He figured it out! Because there is a moment when it ain't money and it ain't status and it ain't who's toughest that matters. What matters is that you don't give up.

"So Klavdiev's play speaks to both generations with respectability and shows that common ground exists between the Soviet generation and today's 'lost' youth."

"I'm impressed. Has he written anything else?"

Zu smiled broadly and replied, "I kept that surprise for last."

"Surprise?"

"Yeah. Several months ago I emailed the department chair here proposing a production of Klavdiev's one-act play *The Polar Truth*, which I had just seen staged in repertory in Saint Petersburg. After a quick read and some back and forth, she approved the project for this coming year's lineup. A graduate student will be directing an undergraduate cast, and I will be heading up the dramaturgy team developing the cast packet and the program notes."

"Congrats, Zu! I'll be front-row center opening night, I promise you. And if this play carries a punch anything like the *Gunner*, it will be a great night. So what's it about?"

"Other neglected social issues plaguing Russia: heroin addiction and an HIV/AIDS epidemic. You see, heroin came home with the troops fleeing Afghanistan. Russian youth were an easy target for addiction. The Soviet Union was falling apart. The economy was collapsing. Unemployment was high. All the Western influences were flowing in through the porous borders and the free press—fashion, music, and, of course, drugs. It was only a matter of time before heroin addiction crossed paths with HIV. In three years the number of drug-related HIV cases skyrocketed from near zero to over sixty percent. And the government's strategy to combat the problem? Neglect. Indifference. Denial. Scorn."

"So we have more outcasts, huh?"

"Yeah. Forced to retreat from society, exiled to a frozen hell on earth. Norilsk, the second-largest city within the Artic Circle, once a Gulag under Stalin and now one of the most polluted places in the world thanks to a smelting plant there they've ironically named 'Hope.'"

"A harsh reality demands a raw play."

"And that's exactly what Klavdiev gives you in *The Polar Truth*. It's what they call a verbatim play. He developed the dialogue from interviews he conducted with the HIV-infected population while visiting there."

"So this hellhole, this Norilsk, is the setting for *The Polar Truth*?"

"Yeah. Klavdiev describes it as a 'whole heat pipe city where the homeless always lay around.'"

"Poetry, Zu."

She nodded and added, "A poetry of suffering."

"Bleak."

"But for a time there's hope when these rootless wanderers become a family."

"But only for a time, right?"

Zulu remained expressionless. She didn't want to give away the store. Instead she said, "Tapeworm stands in a circle of light. He asks us to search our souls. He says, 'The truth is HIV. Because HIV shows what a person's worth. In real terms. Ask yourself what you'd do if you were going to die in ten years. Your answer to that question will show how much truth you have in you.'"

"Resonates in Russia and with us too."

Zulu nodded. "With all the youth everywhere, but especially with us, Casey J. These plays speak to us, to our insecurities, loneliness, isolation. The desire for love, the search for our own identities while fighting off everyone else's attempts to define us, label us, stigmatize us. Natasha Banina says, 'I want real love. I want a bridal veil and chocolate candies. And I want all the girls following us in a line and I want 'em all dying of envy.' I feel that way, Casey J., and I know you do too. I know you do."

I nodded and briefly turned away, fighting back tears. Thankfully the lights began flashing, signaling it was now fifteen minutes until closing. I used the fortuitous interruption to change the subject. "So, Zu, now that you're back, what are your plans? Going to join me again at Headquarters?"

She shook her head and said, "Afraid not this time, Casey J. Believe I should stay at home with my parents. Right after I left for Russia, my father found a lump on his neck while shaving. Thought it was nothing. Swollen gland, maybe a cyst. But later on he learned it was a lot worse. Metastatic squamous neck cancer. The cells start someplace else in the body, break off, and migrate to the lymph nodes."

"Geez, Zu, I'm sorry. Is there anything they can do for him?"

"The doctors have run every test imaginable trying to locate the primary tumor, but they haven't found it. My father joined a clinical trial for a new type of chemotherapy. Finished the chemo regimen and followed that up with radiation. He seemed to be getting better—the tumor shrank—but now he seems to be going downhill again. So while I'd love to be back at Headquarters with you, I think it's best I stay at home, help my mother, and spend some quality time with my dad. God only knows how long he has."

During our walk over to her place, Zu steered the conversation away from her father and herself and back again to the New Drama. But did she really? I remember one thing in particular, not only because of what she said, but how she said it. Zulu glanced over and whispered with conviction, "The social issues depicted, they'll warp and fade over time for sure. They're just the theatrical veneer. But the thought driving these plays, driving this dramaturgy of pain, will survive. It will continue telling our story, our struggle, Casey J. Yours, mine, and theirs."

After dropping Zulu off, I walked back to Headquarters, sat down on the front stoop, and gazed out at the sweep of stars burnishing the midnight sky. I loosened the reins, allowing my mind to explore the future. Would the gods dare be so calculating? Would they dare plant a cancerous seed and argue the ends justify the means? Would they dare sacrifice this small cog to ensure Zulu never came back? Would they dare plot to keep this place free and clear to house a larger mission?

16

I SENSED SOMETHING WAS UP when the silk tie, fedora, and three-piece suit slid into the seat across the booth from me. He didn't say anything. He just kept gazing into my eyes as he reached into his right coat pocket and slipped a folded piece of paper across the table for me to read. I opened the note and stared at the one phrase printed on the paper. My heart sank. It was my deep web ID, "thndrw00d7."

The stranger continued staring into my eyes as he reached into his left coat pocket and slid another folded note across the table. I opened it and mistakenly felt relieved. It was the nick for a fellow hacker I had met online at one of the deep web hacking channels. "You're Nachash?" I asked, my voice rising in excitement. "You're the Serpent?"

The fellow remained pokerfaced as he removed his hat, stroked his bald head, and answered in a rich baritone drawl, "I prefer 'Shiny One' instead." He then reached into his breast pocket, slid a thin leather wallet across the table, and motioned for me to open it. The gold badge on the left read "U.S. Secret Service Special Agent." The photo ID on the right read "Brian R. Beale. Cybercrime Investigative Unit." Fear surged through my body like I had never felt before. I didn't dare look up. I just kept staring down at the shiny badge.

As the agent reached across the table to retrieve his wallet, he offered reassurance with a caveat: "Everything will be just fine as long as you cooperate. You understand?"

I nodded and mumbled, "Yes, sir."

"So how about I pick up your tab here and we head over to your place on Jackson so we can talk a little more freely. You okay with that, Jason?"

I shuddered, nodded again, and repeated, "Yes, sir."

When we got over to Outcast Headquarters, Special Agent Beale stood in the living room, scanned the space, and said, "I'm pretty familiar with the layout here, but I'd still like a walk-through, if you don't mind."

I stared out through a side window to avoid eye contact and replied, "No problem, sir."

He put his hand on my shoulder and said, "Since we're going to be on the same team, Jason, I suggest we get on a first-name basis. So call me Brian."

I looked up and stammered, "Yes, Mr., ah... I mean... Brian."

"So how about that fifty-cent tour, starting with the outside and working our way in?"

I nodded and guided him around back to the fenced-in yard. While slowly circling the house, the agent asked a series of questions about the neighbors and the boundary lines and added several observations to a small notebook. As we reentered the house through the front door, I finally sucked up enough courage to stand in the middle of the living room, extend my arms, and declare, "Pretty much what you see here is what you get. And as you probably already know, it's an open floor plan down here on the first floor, with the dining area back there just beyond the half wall."

"You mind if we take a look?" he asked.

"No problem, Mr., ah… Sorry. No problem, Brian."

When we reached the kitchen, the agent immediately moved over to a closed door and probed, "So what's in here, Jason?"

"Steps leading downstairs," I said. "I've only been down there a couple of times. Kinda damp and close. No windows."

"So what do we have? A cellar or an unfinished basement?"

"I don't know what you'd call it. Something in between the two, I guess."

"Is there any way out down there?"

I desperately tried making a joke. "One way in, no way out. Just like the cemetery."

He ignored my attempt at humor, whipped out a penlight, and said, "So why don't we have a look?"

"No problem, ah… Brian."

He disappeared down the stairs but returned in a flash and said, "Okay, so you ready to continue the tour upstairs?"

"Oh, there's not much to see up there since my roommates moved out."

I began trembling again as I overheard him whisper under his breath, "I beg to differ with you on that one, young man."

After inspecting the bath and three empty bedrooms, we moved over to the inner sanctum. I pointed to the locked door and said sheepishly, "My bedroom."

He nodded and asked, "Mind if we have a look? You have a key?"

"Ah… ah… no problem," I stammered while plumbing the depths of my jeans pockets. "Here it is." I unlocked the door, flipped the switch, and began swooping up a week's worth of clothes I had shed all over the floor. "Come on in, but watch your step. It's been kind of crazy around here. You know, with finals and everything."

"No problem, Jason. I was an underclassman too not so many years ago." He glanced around the room—first, at the photographs and models of the *Titanic*; next at the floor-to-ceiling rack of legacy computer equipment; and then at the hundreds of vinyls stacked in the corner and on the window bench. He then moved over to my computer, rested his hands on the back of the desk chair, and said, "You mind if we have a look?"

I shook my head, sat down at the computer, and fired it up. When the home page appeared, the agent asked, "You mind if I take a seat?"

I swallowed hard, nodded, and pushed back from the desk. He sat down and began flipping through screens, running some sort of diagnostics Stats would have known, whereas I didn't have a clue about it. I flopped down in my leather chair and watched helplessly as he drilled, clawed, and dug his way through the operating system and every application. After about fifteen minutes of probing, he mumbled something to the effect, "So that's what you've done."

He swung around in the chair and said, "I've got to hand it to you, Jason, that's pretty damn clever. The boys back East are going to be impressed with this. You know, we've been in your system off and on for months watching you harden your defenses, making it tougher for us to crack in all the time. But when we saw you managing to keep us out for weeks on end, we knew we had to make a move and lock you down. In fact, I just got word from our gurus late last night that they had finally managed to hack into your latest network update."

A thought flashed through my head, "If his boys did what I think they did, I have an opportunity here to make a friend for life!" I stood up and asked, "You mind if I take a look there?"

The agent pushed back from the desk, stood up, and said dryly, "No problem. She's all yours, Jason."

I sat down, quickly got back to the home page, and launched Thunderwood 7.0. The agent was telling the truth. His boys had managed to crack in through the honeypot and tripped the alert function. My heart was beating a mile a minute now as I checked the live system for exploits. No footprints. Everything was safe and sound. It was the fourth of July on the sixth of June as fireworks arced and exploded in my head. It was now my time to swing around in *my* chair and announce to Special Agent Beale that his "gurus" back East had made a big mistake. But I asked coolly, "So you say your boys hacked into the system last night?"

"Yep," he said, without looking up. He was examining one of my models of the *Titanic*.

"You sure?" I tweaked.

"Yep."

I continued drilling. "Well, I don't see anything here."

"They're good, Jason. They're real good. They're clean in and then clean out."

"But maybe not as good as—"

That last punch I pulled was just enough to get his attention. He moved over to the computer and signaled for me to get up and out of the way. He immediately sat down and began flipping through various screens. And after letting him twist in the wind for about five minutes, I finally offered to cut him down. "I think I can resolve our problem, Brian."

He slowly swung around in the chair and asked, "How's that?"

"Let me get a pen and legal pad. I'll show you."

With pen in hand, I drew two circles side by side and explained what was happening. "Okay, you're here in the left circle. Your techies said they had hacked into a network. They were right. They had. But they had cracked into the circle on the right, not the one over here on the left where you are. Now, your techies honestly thought they had hacked into your left circle, when in fact they had only exploited the one on the right here. You see what I'm saying? While you're in the real network, they're lurking about in a virtual network mistakenly thinking they're in the live system."

The agent jumped up from his chair and motioned for me to sit down. "Here. Show me in real time what you're talking about."

I toggled over into Thunderwood 7.0, pulled up the alert activity screen, and pointed to the flag indicating an intrusion in the virtual system late the previous evening. "You see, there's a record here of the alarm they set off last night." I then toggled back and forth between the two systems, demonstrating how they were the same in every respect except for one—the honeypot I had planted to lure intruders into the virtual system.

"Okay, Jason, so I now know what happened, but tell me how you managed to pull it off."

"I developed a piece of 'recreational software,'" I explained, "Thunderwood 7.0, and loaded it onto the computer here. As you can see, it works by creating a parallel network on a virtual machine. Before anyone gets into the live system, they must first be vetted by moving through the virtual network. If they are good guys, they are passed along to the live system. If they're bad guys, they stay put in the virtual network thinking they're lurking around in the real McCoy. Thunderwood 7.0 then tips me off that they're in the virtual system, where I can monitor their movement, tag their addresses, and put them in the crosshairs to deliver a lethal counterattack."

The agent shook his head, flashed a smile for the first time, and said, "Man, oh man, you've got some serious shit going down here, Jason."

Sensing an opening, I began probing. "So, Brian… ah, you mind if I ask what this is about? You said something about our being on the same team and on a first-name basis if I cooperated."

"Fair enough, Jason." He paused, carefully considering his words, and then said, "Well, let me put it to you this way. I can tell you what it *was* about; but after seeing your software, I think this has escalated well beyond my pay grade. But the long and the short of it is, we've been surveilling you and your former roommate, Kevin, ever since you fellows cropped up on the deep web hacking sites. You must have known we would be tailing you."

I shook my head and responded honestly, "I didn't really give it any thought, since we weren't doing anything illegal."

"It's not always the action, Jason, but sometimes the perception that's enough to get someone's attention. I'm sure you've heard the old adages, 'Birds of a feather' and 'Where there's smoke.'"

I nodded.

"So the deep web led us back here to your network and your friendly competition with Kevin. And as I said, we've been watching you get increasingly better at defending your system against Kevin's attacks."

I shuddered at the implication of his revelation and interrupted, "Is Kevin in any trouble?"

The agent shook his head and replied, "What's that famous Wayne line from *Iwo Jima*? 'Life is tough, but it's tougher if you're stupid.' So life won't get any tougher for Kevin unless he does something stupid. You understand?"

I nodded again.

"Listen up, Jason. Kevin doesn't know we've been tracking y'all, and he doesn't know anything about you and me today. And I needn't have to remind you that this meeting is totally off the record. You do understand there will be serious consequences if you utter a word about our conversation today?"

"Yes, sir. But I still don't have a clue what I'm *not* supposed to be talking about."

"Retail point-of-sale systems."

I shrugged. "POS systems?"

"Yep. After watching you get increasingly better at defending your network, we figured you could probably help us solve the POS issue. There's a growing number of retail data breaches across the world, with millions of credit and debit cards being compromised."

"If you don't mind my asking, how are they cracking in?"

"You know the drill, Jason. Any way they can. Stolen vendor credentials, unsecured ports, outdated operating systems and applications, and on and on. And once the perps are in, they make a beeline for the security and payments system, which interfaces with the POS terminals at the retail sites. As you probably know, every time you swipe your credit or debit card at the cash register to authorize your purchase, the information encoded on the magnetic stripe—cardholder's name, card number, expiration date, and the like—it's all transmitted from the POS terminal to the central payment application and then on to the retailer's payment-processing vendor."

"I see where you're going there," I said, "but the transferred data are encrypted… right?"

"Yes and no. The customer data are encrypted when they leave the POS terminal on the way to the central payment system and then again when the data leave the retailer's network for the payment processor's system. But there's a point when the customer data are stored in the system's RAM in plaintext, and that's when the malware, a RAM scraper, can read and capture the customer data."

"Clever."

"Oh, it's nothing new, but this type of exploit's gaining in popularity with these lowlifes. It sure has gotten our attention. A lot of bad stuff can happen before companies realize they've been hacked. On average only twenty-five to thirty percent of companies discover their own breaches. And for retailers, self-discovery is down somewhere in the five to ten percent range. That means these retail hacks can go on for months on end before they are uncovered."

"Can we back up a minute?"

"Sure, what is it?"

"So I understand the breach, the capture, and the storage of the customer data on a compromised retail server, but how do the hackers move the data from there back to their home base?"

"An elegantly planned escape route, if I must say so. They upload C2 and exfiltrate malware onto the compromised system."

"I'm sorry, C2 and exfiltrate malware? What's that?"

"It's malware that's designed to gain command and control remotely, and then export captured data out of the retailer automatically, post exploit."

"Okay, so the data then go back to the hackers' home base, right?"

The agent shook his head. "No, remember I said '*elegantly planned* escape route.' These boys like to use staging areas in the States as an intermediate stop before bringing the data all the way back to home base. You know, a way to cover their tracks. First, they move the outbound data to three or four compromised FTP servers scattered throughout the US. They usually export these data during the middle of the day to bury the transfer in the routine traffic of a regular business day. And then later they transfer the stolen card information from the FTP servers back to wherever home is."

"Any idea who's behind this?"

"A postmortem of the malware code provides some clues. For example, we found some Russian slang and some passwords. One of them was Bloody0888. In the Ukraine, August 4, 1988, is known as 'Bloody Thursday,' the day the police forcibly broke up a large demonstration supporting Perestroika. Bloody0888 also happens to be the nick for an online gamer sitting atop an Internet leaderboard. And there's another name buried in the exfiltrate code: Sandokan."

"Sandokan?"

"Yep. The lead pirate in Salgari's novel, *The Tigers of Mompracem*. Sandokan's a known alias for a Ukrainian dealer trafficking in stolen credit card numbers. His online card number sites use country domains of places like Laos, Russia, and Somalia. So when you add all of the clues up, you can make a reasonable assumption these RAM scrapers are operating out of Treasure Island."

"Treasure Island?"

"Our name internally for Odessa, the jewel of the Black Sea and home to the largest underground syndicate of carders."

"Sounds like it would be easy to take them down with everything you know about them."

"It's not as easy as you think. The ringleaders never meet. They don't even know each other's names. And every communication between them is anonymous and way off the grid." The agent paused, checked his watch, and said, "Hey, Jason, I've got to get out of here. But remember, it's business as usual and today never happened. You clear on that?"

I nodded and said, "Yes, I understand. So when will I see you again?"

"I'm not sure you ever will."

"I don't understand."

"Remember what I said earlier? I said I was going to tell you what it *was* about; but after having seen your software, I believe this operation has escalated well beyond my pay grade. So, hold tight, Jason. Someone will be in touch." He extended his hand and said, "Good to see you, Thunderwood 7."

"Same here, Nachash."

And as the agent stepped out into the hallway, he turned around, raised his fedora exposing his bald head, and said, "Remember now, I'd prefer 'Shiny One' to 'The Serpent' any day."

I nodded and then stood motionless in the last light of a dying day.

17

A BREATHY, UPBEAT ACCENT CALLED out lightheartedly, "He's moved over to this side now one branch higher." I peered out from behind the enormous trunk, spotted the kitten, and then tried unsuccessfully to locate the sultry voice below. Taking great care not to fall to my death, I maneuvered to the other side of the trunk, sneaked up behind the kitten, and managed to grasp him gently by the nape of the neck.

"Good job!" the accent shouted. "I'd hire you in an instant!"

While continuing to hug the tree with one arm and holding the kitten in the other, I began my slow descent toward the large limb closest to the ground. And after I managed to ease down onto the branch and straddle it without sacrificing my manhood, a hand shot up through the thick foliage and moved from side to side, clutching the air. The unfamiliar voice rang out again: "Here, pass that bad boy down to me."

I handed my pride and joy over to this invisible stranger, then quickly swung my left leg up and over the limb, dropped to the ground, and stood facing one of the most striking women I had ever seen. This tall, lithe ebony beauty had a deep, rich complexion; large, brown, almond-shaped eyes; full lips; high cheekbones; and silky black hair—one half cornrowed, the other half loose—flowing casually over to the right side in an over-the-shoulder ponytail with the ends curled and fluffed. She was wearing curve-hugging jeans, leather T-strap sandals, and a red floral camisole with ruffled hem and spaghetti straps.

This exotic beauty was holding *my* kitten close to her full, rounded breasts, stroking his purring head, and flashing a smile that radiated an intense glow from within. Just as I was about to open the conversation, the backhoe and jackhammer revved up again less than a hundred feet away. The startled kitten jumped and tried clawing his way up and over her shoulder, but this mysterious stranger knew exactly how to calm the little guy's fears and gently regain control. I shrugged, smiled, and pointed to the pathway leading up to Headquarters. She nodded and began walking slowly toward the house. I fell in behind her on the narrow path and marveled at that "brave vibration each way free."

When we reached the porch, we sat down on the top step side by side. I pointed out toward the construction and said, "The noise is what got this all started. When they fired up the equipment this morning, my kitten jumped a foot in the air and then ran straight up the trunk there. I'm really glad you came along to help us out."

"No problem. But say, you have any idea why they're digging up the pavement everywhere?"

I nodded. "Yeah, I asked one of the crew last week. He said they were replacing the old cable with newer, high-speed fiber optics."

"It's progress, but it's still a mess. They've got everything ripped out from here all the way over to campus. You lost your service?"

"Yeah, once, but they'd warned us of the outage in advance."

When the small talk ran out, I extended my hand and said, "Sorry. I'm Jason Lynch."

The young woman laughed, shook my hand, and said, "Ivory Eboué. Nice to meet you, Jason." She raised my kitten off her lap, rubbed noses with it, and said, "While we're doing introductions, what's the big fellow's name?"

"Well, that's a funny story in itself. I first thought of Jock."

She laughed. "Jock? Because of his athleticism?"

"Hey, that's pretty funny. But no. Winston Churchill loved cats, and Jock was his favorite. Here he was, the most powerful wartime prime minister of Great Britain, but he wouldn't eat supper without Jock dining with him. In fact, Churchill was so fond of his furry sidekick that he asked that an orange tiger with a white bib and four white socks always live in his historic country home at Chartwell, Kent. After Churchill's death—and Jock was there on the bed right beside him when he died—the curators honored Churchill's wishes. And I read they just installed the latest Jock last month. I believe they're up to number six now."

"Well, I see why you considered the name. Your marmalade tabby here sporting the white collar and paws would surely be on the short list to be Jock VII." After sharing a good laugh, she asked, "But if not Jock, what then?"

"So after rejecting Jock as too British for my all-American guy, I next considered Chaplain."

"After Charlie Chaplain, the Little Tramp?"

"Yeah, in a roundabout way. The name Chaplain is short-hand for Hart Crane's poem 'Chaplainesque,' which depicts the Little Tramp finding a stray kitten in the streets. You see, when my roommates left me all alone here in this big house after our freshman year, I have to admit it got a bit lonely sometimes. During my sophomore year, I had stumbled on Crane's poem in a literature course. And then it hit me! Why not cure my isolation with a rescue kitten? You know, orphan ships passing in the night. A win-win for him and me. So having heard the famished kitten in the wilderness, I rushed over to the animal shelter, saw this fellow's soulful eyes peering out of his cage at me, and whispered to him, 'From now on it's gonna be you and me—you and me against the world.'"

"But you didn't stick with Chaplain either, did you?"

I shook my head and smiled. "No. Another name came to mind."

She lifted the kitten off her lap again, held him out at arm's length, and said, "Since your owner's playing hide-and-seek, how about you telling me your name?" She then drew him in close to her ear, as if ready to receive his secret.

I playfully leaned in behind the kitten and whispered, "My name's Geb."

She immediately responded, directing the question to the kitten. "After the French writer, Émile Gebhart? Or are we dealing with an acronym here?"

I froze. While she rubbed noses with Geb again, I just sat there staring at her profile and thinking, "Ivory's the one. Ivory's the one."

She shook Geb gently and said, "Now stop teasing me, big fellow. Is it the writer or the book?"

I leaned in behind the kitten again and answered with a question, "Your earrings. Fractal ferns?"

She slowly lowered the kitten onto her lap and gazed silently but knowingly into my eyes. In a matter of minutes we had moved from meaningless banter to meaningful dialogue, from axiom to proof, from Russell and Whitehead to an unprovable truth.

She smiled and nodded. "The earrings were a birthday gift from my father."

"Sounds like there's a story there," I probed.

"I suppose.... Do you really want to hear it?"

"Of course. I wouldn't have asked if I didn't."

"Well, I guess it really all began when I was seven or eight. For my First Communion my father gave me a Bible and *Gödel, Escher, Bach*, which he then kept for safekeeping until we came to America. On my twelfth birthday he returned *GEB*; and every year after that, he's given me earrings in various geometric shapes. As he presents them, he assigns each pair a name, like 'fractal ferns,' 'Koch's snowflakes,' 'Serpinski's triangles,' 'Mandlebrot's sets,' 'strange loops,' and the like."

"Your father sounds, ah, really unique. If you don't mind my asking, what does he do?"

"He's now a professor emeritus of mathematics here at Pantheon. Still doing research. Harmonic analysis—you know, Fourier transforms, quantum mechanics, momentum space wave functions."

I didn't have a clue, so I nodded and said, "I see." I dusted myself off and quickly tacked to another topic. "You said 'until we came to America.' Where was home before you came to the States?"

"Africa. The Ivory Coast."

"When did you guys leave?"

"After the rebellion. For the most part everything had been pretty stable in my country while Houphouët-Boigny was president—both economically and politically."

"When was that?" I asked.

"From the sixties to the early nineties. But after he died, everything went south, as you like to say. We had a constitutional coup d'état, a military coup d'état, ethnic massacres, a recession, inflation, and then all-out civil war in 2002. That's when my father announced we were leaving."

"Was your father a professor in your homeland?"

She nodded. "He had been on the faculty at the University of Abidjan before becoming the director of the IRMA."

"The IRMA?"

"Sorry. The Abidjan Mathematical Research Institute."

"So your family arrived in '02?"

"Ah, no. It was a little later. I remember we flew out on the winter solstice, stayed several weeks in Paris, and arrived in the States in January. So it would have been very early '03."

"You come here to McGill directly after getting to the States?"

"No, my father had a research and teaching position in Pittsburgh before coming here to Pantheon."

"What about the rest of your family? Any brothers or sisters?"

Ivory shook her head and joked, "No. Just me. One of a kind."

"Your mother?"

"She's much younger than my father. She still teaches. Teaches French at McGill High."

"And what about this one of a kind? You said you'd hire me in an instant? You own a company?"

She laughed aloud and said, "No, no. Just weekend manager at the McGill Veterinary Hospital. I'm full-time at Pantheon. A senior."

"Major in mathematics?"

She shook her head.

"French?"

She shook her head again and said, "I had to find my own sandbox. I'm premed."

I smiled. "I should have picked up on the clues—working at the vet's office and seeing how easily you hit it off with Geb here." I then held my breath as I waited, hoping for a positive answer to my next question. "You and your parents plan on staying in the States for good?"

"One thing about us, Jason, we don't look back. We all have permanent residence status and are in the final stages of getting our citizenship. So it looks like you'll have to put up with us from here on out." She paused, touched my arm, and said,

"That's enough about me. How about you? Will the real Jason Lynch please stand up!"

I tried hiding my nervousness. I was way outside my comfort zone. People, and especially beautiful women, never showed interest or asked personal questions of this perennial outcast. I stared down at my Chuck Taylor All-Stars and mumbled, "Not much to say, Ivory. McGill Elementary, Middle, and High. Sophomore this past year at Pantheon. Currently majoring in computer science."

"Any brothers or sisters?"

I shook my head and took a shot at some lame humor. "No, same as you. They broke the mold after I was born."

"Your mother and father. What do they do?"

"They're both writers. My mother's a novelist. My father composes songs."

"I read a lot. What's your mother's name? Maybe I've heard of her."

"Maybe. Her name is Danielle de Silva."

"*The* Danielle de Silva?"

I nodded.

"No way! I don't believe it! I've read several of your mother's novels, *A Time Outside the Days*, *My Brother's Wife*, and *The Afterlife*. She's signed every one of my copies, Jason. That's unbelievable! You must be very proud. She's really a great writer. But I'm curious. Have you read all of them?"

I nodded. "Of course." I paused, smiled broadly, and added, "You know, it was required reading from the core curriculum." I paused again and then asked, "You have a favorite, Ivory?"

"Hmm... let's see. As I said, I've liked them all; but if I were forced to choose one, I guess it would be *My Brother's Wife*."

"Why's that?"

"Oh, on one level I'd have to say it was Evan and Addison's defiance of social norms—staying together after learning they shared a father; building a future by trying to restore the past, you know, trying to return their plantation to its glory years; and then unconditionally loving their wayward son, Gabriel, who runs away at sixteen never to be seen again."

"You said on one level. You think there's more than one?"

She nodded. "Yeah, I believe so. I think *My Brother's Wife* is a modern retelling of Paradise after the fall. Here the names are switched. Adam become Addison and Eve becomes Evan. The plantation is the Garden of Eden, and Gabriel is their errant son, Cain, whom God condemns to become 'a fugitive and a vagabond in the earth.'"

I didn't dare plumb the depths for a third level for fear Ivory might begin to piece together rumors about my parents' past. Some twenty years ago salacious stories traveled far and wide about their incestuous relationship. If Ivory were to have ever stumbled upon any of them, she would have begun to realize there is indeed a third, autobiographical level buried beneath the first two layers and that she had now come face-to-face with that wanderer, that outcast whom the gods had condemned to roam the earth. So I shrugged my shoulders and said, "I guess we'll have to leave your interpretation for you and my mother to hash out over dinner sometime in the near future."

She understood the meaning in my words and replied, "I'd like that, Jason. I'd like that very much."

Sensing it was time to tack away from the shoals again, I said, "Would you and Geb like to come inside away from the dust and noise for a cup of coffee or herbal tea?"

She smiled and teased, "I'm sure Geb would. But I'll have to take a rain check. I'm filling in for a sick employee at the vet's a half hour from now."

After rubbing noses with Geb one more time and handing him over to me, Ivory stood up and said, "It was really nice meeting you, Jason."

"Same here, Ivory. Ah, by the way, I'd like to keep in touch."

"That's easy. My student address is Ivorye@pantheon.edu."

"I'll email you later this week," I said, as I gently deposited Geb inside the front door, far away from the roaring equipment at the end of the path.

After stepping out beyond the construction, Ivory winked and said, "Look forward to hearing from you, Jason." She turned and began walking slowly up the tree-lined street toward town center. I moved out into the middle of Jackson Avenue and watched her recede into the camouflage trunks of the narrowing sycamores. I smiled appreciatively and began humming an old lyric: "I hate seein' ya go, babe, but I sure *love* watchin' ya leave."

18

DESPITE A LEAD-PIPE CINCH prediction, the fedora and the Tidewater drawl were back. As Special Agent Beale slid into the booth across the table from me, he said, "Good to see you, Thunderwood."

"Same here, Nachash. But what gives? I thought I had seen the last of you months ago. You know, you said I was way above your pay grade and all that."

He smiled and responded without giving away the store. "The boss was generous. I got a good raise. So here, let me get your tab, and let's get over to Jackson Avenue so I can bring you up to speed."

As we climbed out of his rental in front of Headquarters, a second vehicle pulled up behind us. Three young, muscular men sporting buzz cuts piled out onto the sidewalk. They were all wearing T-shirts, jeans, and hiking boots. Each was carrying a large canvas backpack and a duffel. Special Agent Beale turned and motioned for me to take the lead up the front path and for the young men to follow on behind us.

When we got into the house, the agent made the introductions. To this day I'm not quite sure he wasn't pulling my leg. He introduced them as "Rich," "Henry," and "Thomas," which I knew could easily be reduced to the common nicknames "Tom, Dick, and Harry." We then moved back into the dining area, pulled chairs up to the table, and sat quietly while Special Agent Beale began filling me in. "Suffice it to say, Jason, Homeland, the Pentagon, and the CIA were impressed with your software. They want us to make some tweaks and then begin pilot testing as soon as we can get everything squared away here."

"Regional or national retail chains?" I asked.

The agent laughed and replied, "Hey, Jason, remember I told you I got a pay raise. We've moved well beyond twenty-one. We're now playing high-stakes poker."

"I don't understand. You said Thunderwood was ideal for addressing the point-of-sale systems issue. So if that's twenty-one, what's high-stakes poker?"

"Protecting the grid."

"The grid?"

"Yep. The US national power grid, Jason. All of it—three regional grids, thirty-two hundred distribution utilities, fifty-five thousand electric substations, four hundred and fifty thousand miles of high-voltage transmission lines. It's a big fucking deal, Jason, and it's up to the five of us sitting here at this table on Jackson Avenue to make sure nothing ever happens to it. Think of it. Just a few years ago on a hot summer day several high-voltage lines in Ohio rubbed up against overgrown trees and shut the system down. The alarm in the local utility failed to sound, and parts of the grid in southeastern Canada and eight northeastern states began failing. And what do we get for several sagging power lines? Fifty million people losing power for two days. Eleven or more people dying. And the economy bleeding six billion dollars. Now think of a prolonged outage over an even wider area, and what do you have? A hundred million or more in the dark for months on end and a profound impact on the food and water supply, health care, communications, emergency response, the economy, and even national defense.

"And who's going to protect the grid? Congress? Federal government agencies? The state public utilities commissions? The privately owned utilities, which comprise ninety percent of the total grid? When everyone's in charge, Jason, no one's in control. Hell, they've all known about the vulnerabilities for decades now, and they've done virtually nothing about it."

I eased my hand into the air and said, "Excuse me, ah, Brian. I have a question. I don't understand. How are the five of us here supposed to stop a nuclear blast, an electromagnetic pulse attack launched by a rogue nation?"

"It's a real threat, Jason, but a real threat only in the long run. For now, an electromagnetic pulse attack is a head fake. It gets a lot of attention in the press because it's sensational. It grabs headlines, drives web traffic, attracts advertising bucks. But the enemy's smarter than that, Jason. They don't want to be annihilated any more than we do. Plus they want to stay under the radar and maintain their deniability."

"So what kind of attack are we most likely dealing with here?"

"Our analysts have come up with potential scenarios based on perceived vulnerabilities in the overall grid. Let's start with large generating plants. The bad news: if terrorists target these huge generators, we could lose hundreds of gigawatts of capacity in one fell swoop. The good news: most, if not all, of these nuclear, coal, and gas facilities are heavily protected.

"Okay, let's move on to the four hundred and fifty thousand miles of high-voltage transmission lines. The bad news: they're obviously easy targets. The good news: they're relatively easy to replace, and we have a lot of experience dealing with downed power lines caused by tornadoes, hurricanes, ice storms, and the like. The enemy could indeed cause outages, but they would most likely be of short duration with minimal impact. Disruptive but not catastrophic.

"Now let's look at the substations, which have been under scrutiny since the early nineties. The bad news: substations are high-value targets, and they continue to remain vulnerable to attack. You knock some of the these babies out and you're going to be subsisting without power for some time. They are not easy to replace. The good news: the boys back East are aware of the vulnerability to physical attack and have now begun in earnest to work the problem. And then finally, we have the control centers and the supervisory control and data acquisition systems, which are critical to the flow of power throughout the regional grids. The bad news: cracking into several of these networks could cause a big-time power failure. The good news: thanks to you, Jason, cybersecurity may actually be our strongest suit. "So the bottom line: while the boys in Virginia and Maryland are working out strategies to protect transmission and distribution substations from physical strikes, 'The Jackson Avenue Five' here will be developing and implementing software to thwart a cyberattack. Everyone clear on that?"

The four of us at the table nodded and mumbled, "Yes, sir."

"Okay, then. But before we get started, let's review a little more background." He paused and glanced at his notes before continuing. "So our analysts believe the enemy's taking its cue from operation 'Olympic Games.'"

"And what's that?" I asked.

"Allegedly an American and Israeli operation to attack Iran's nuclear enrichment program. I use the term 'allegedly' since we've never confirmed we played a role in the mission. So you hear officials say, 'I can neither confirm nor deny our participation in launching the Stuxnet offensive.'"

"But you do know how it worked, right?"

"Sure, it's no real secret. The Stuxnet worm captured the controllers running Iran's nuclear centrifuges and caused the centrifuges to spin out of control."

"So is the Stuxnet worm the world's cyber weapon of choice now?"

"No, but the current nemesis, Snake, is comparable in complexity to the worm."

I smiled. "Hmm," I said. "Interesting. Now who would be more likely tasked with killing the Snake than another? The enemy has their Snake, but we have our Serpent." I raised my hands in a mock defense. "I know, I know, you prefer the alternate translation but…"

Special Agent Beale peered over his glasses and didn't crack a smile. I leaned back in my chair, embarrassed. "Sorry, sir. There's just a lot of pressure."

He nodded and responded, "Apology accepted, Jason. Any more questions before we move on?"

"Yes, sir. Can you tell me, what do we know about this Snake malware?"

"We think it's an upgrade to the cyber espionage tool kit, Agent.BTZ, which penetrated the Pentagon's classified systems in '08. Our analyses indicate Snake's been in the works for going on six or seven years and is too complex to have been written by a lone wolf or a nonstate entity. There's no question in our minds it's state sponsored. The architecture has about fifty submodules, giving the malware significant flexibility and the capacity to become increasingly complex over time. Snake started out primarily as an espionage tool, but it now appears to create pathways for other malware to be loaded onto compromised networks. You know, penetrate, reconnoiter, and then launch an attack. It's really nasty stuff."

"So if it's state sponsored, whom do you think's behind it?"

"Well, first, we think the programmers were working in a GMT+4 time zone, which would include Moscow. And secondly, there are bits of Russian text scattered throughout the code. So I'll let you do the math on that one." He scanned the room and addressed his next question to all of us at the table. "Before we move on, is everyone clear on the background information?"

Everyone at the table nodded and mumbled again, "Yes, sir."

"Okay. So let's discuss housekeeping issues for Jackson Avenue. Thomas, Henry, and Rich will be moving in this week and taking the three unoccupied bedrooms upstairs. They'll be working with you, Jason, on installing equipment and making enhancements to Thunderwood 7.0."

I raised my hand and asked hesitantly, "Ah, sorry, sir, but did anyone run this by my landlord, Mr. Sengel? You see, the deal my father and he worked out was that, one, we would be renting the entire house, two, I couldn't sublet, three, no one else was allowed to live on the premises under any circumstances, and four, if I violated the rules, I was out of here."

Special Agent Beale flashed a half smile and replied, "You don't have to worry, Jason. Everything's taken care of. Mr. Sengel doesn't own the property anymore."

"Say again."

"Mr. Sengel doesn't own it anymore."

"Who does?"

"You, me, and three hundred million other people, Jason. The boys back East bought the hacienda for us several months ago." He paused, glanced at his notes again, and continued. "As far as the layout here, we won't be making many changes to the upstairs, but this floor and the basement will be undergoing major overhauls beginning next week. Once we complete the construction down cellar, we can then begin installing the network and computer cluster. And according to my Gantt chart here, work on the satellite dishes and the underground cables running from here out to the new fiber optics on Jackson will start day after tomorrow."

I couldn't hold back. "You guys are responsible for all the construction from here over to the university these past few months, aren't you?"

The agent flashed another half smile and replied, "Now doesn't that make you feel special?"

"Unfuckingbelievable," I whispered.

"Which now brings me to security," he said, picking up the thread. "First of all, if anyone asks about all the changes going on around here, just say that the new landlord must be getting ready to raise the rent. Next, since we're working in a residential neighborhood, we'll be establishing a soft perimeter. During daylight hours, you guys will see various landscapers, vendors, workers, and the like moving in and out of the area. They and some well-placed cameras will be keeping an eye on things around here. And during the night, what appears to be the local constabulary will be replacing the daytime help and patrolling the neighborhood by car and on foot.

"Now some house policies. We're playing by Vegas rules. What happens here, stays here. Everybody on the same page?"

We all mumbled again, "Yes, sir."

"As far as what you do on your own time in your own bedroom, no one gives a squat. But down here on this floor, we have an undergraduate and three graduate students busting their asses to maintain their GPAs. Are we all clear on that? Everyone got the story straight?"

Everyone nodded.

He then pointed to the basement door and declared, "It should go without saying that under penalty of death no one even entertains *the thought* of taking unauthorized guests downstairs. So are we clear on *that*?"

Reflecting the seriousness of the warning, we all nodded our heads this time and said decisively, "Yes, sir!"

I raised my hand. "Point of order, ah, Brian."

"What is it, Jason?"

"So you're saying I can have anyone over as a guest?"

He nodded his head.

"Even if they're not currently a US citizen?"

And then there was that half smile again. "I would say no, Jason." He paused for effect and then added, "But with one exception: your girlfriend from the Ivory Coast. She and her immediate family are well on their way to citizenship, and they all checked out okay."

I was chagrinned. "Should've known they'd find out about her," I thought.

"Anymore questions?"

We all shook our heads and said, "No, sir."

Special Agent Beale paused, looked each of us in the eye, and whispered, "I know I repeat myself, but this *is* a big fucking deal. And we've really been blessed. Only a few people in their lifetimes will ever have the opportunity we have here—to protect and defend the United States of America. So I ask you, gentlemen, if not us, who? If not now, when?" He scanned the room, pounded the table sharply, and shouted, "Let's roll!"

19

A S THE NEXT STEP in our growing relationship, Ivory invited Geb and me over to her place for a
Saturday evening meal. My nerves jangled as we waited outside
her apartment for the first time. But when our 'African Queen'
opened the door, all of that fear dissipated. We were greeted by
the usual loving smile and a burst of burgundy and gold. But
first things first. Before we could even share an embrace, Ivory
rushed to the canvas carrier, unlatched the door, and lifted "*our*
Geb" into the air. Rubbing noses with the little scene stealer, she
asked, "How's the big fellow doing? You ready for a homemade
treat? You up for some stewed liver and kidneys?" And as she
lowered him gently onto her breast, she turned and motioned
for me to follow *them* into the apartment.

But I guess it's true that patience does have its own rewards.
After releasing the beast into the wild to explore his new surroundings, Ivory extended her arms and pulled me in close
for a warm embrace. She whispered, "I've really missed your
company, Jason, but I know you're doing what you think you
have to do to keep your grades up. I mean, staying in that big
old house cramming day after day."

Feeling uncomfortable, I let that sleeping dog lie. I held her out at arm's length and slowly admired the traditional sarong-like wrap, which she had fashioned from a fabric called *pagne*. The motif of this classic Ivorian wax print comprised alternating burgundy and white bars, with gold latticework overlaying the burgundy and rows of large magenta eyes superimposed on the white stripes.

After our chance meeting outside Headquarters, I had done my due diligence on Ivorian history, art, and culture and learned that some of the classic pagne designs had been given names and that Ivorian women wore the various motifs to communicate their moods and feelings on a host of issues. I gazed into her eyes and asked, "A classic design, right?"

She nodded. "You like it?"

"Yeah, it's provocative. Stimulating. Just like you. And does this particular motif have a name?"

She nodded again. "Several of them. Some call it 'L'Oeil de Boeuf,' or 'the Bull's Eye'; churchgoers know it as 'God's eye'; and others refer to it as 'Lisu ya Pité,' or 'lustful eye,' when the women want their men to know they desire them."

"So what do you call it?" I teased.

She smiled and replied coyly, "How do you say? Oh, yes. That's for me to know and you to find out."

I laughed. "Touché!" I said. "Touché!" I then turned and scanned the living room, which could easily have been mistaken for a world-class gallery. While the desk and end tables featured small Ivorian sculptures made of wood or string, the walls were lined with framed woodcuts, lithographs, wooden ceremonial masks, and even a carved interior door depicting a crocodile basking in a pool of geometric abstractions.

I turned to Ivory and said, "You have a great eye for talent. These pieces are stunning."

"Sorry, but I can't take any of the credit here. They're all on loan from my parents. My mother's the one with the vision. She can spot masterpieces a decade into the future."

I moved over to the desk and examined a foot-high female string figure suspended somewhere between African heritage and contemporary art. Despite her face peeling back from the skull (or was it a mask?), she held her thin, stretched head high and thrust her bony arms to the heavens.

"It's one of my favorite pieces," she said and added, "By Lattier, the 'bare-handed sculptor.' He learned to coax the profound magic out of all things string."

"Picassoesque and yet it retains its African roots. Does it have a name? 'Supplication'? 'Entreaty'? 'Plea'? 'Prayer'?"

She wagged her finger and said with a smile, "There you go again, Jason. No, she's not asking for the pain to stop. In fact, she's overcome it. Lattier called the piece 'Victory.' You see how her arms extend out in a V rather than straight up? That's no accident. Lattier's telegraphing a meaning."

I shook my head and muttered, "I dunno. You and Geb—" Discretion being the better part of valor, I stopped midsentence and turned toward the impressive mask exhibit on the walls. "Did your mother collect these as well?"

Ivory nodded. "Not exactly. She inherited most of them. They've been passed down through her family from one generation to the next."

I pointed toward one of the more startling of the wooden masks featuring painted horns, flared nostrils, bared teeth, and a spotted crocodile clamping down on the belly of a lamb. I sidled up to Ivory and said, "The scary-looking fellow there. Can you fill me in?"

"It's a man's mask, the Bo Nun Amuin. It depicts the sacred bush cow. The men keep these spiritual masks hidden in the African bush away from the women and children. Ivorians believe masks have souls; and when you don one of them, you are allowing the spirit of the mask to enter your body."

I pointed to a quartet of antique masks grouped on the far wall. "Those fellows over there look far less menacing."

"Yes, everyone sees these masks, but only the men can wear them. I remember, as a young girl, seeing them being worn during the Goli ritual of celebration. The masks are danced sequentially."

"What do you mean?"

"Well, the flat, round, horned mask there in the top left corner appears first during the ceremony. It represents younger males. It's called a Kplekple. The one there at top right, the complex, three-dimensional one—"

"What is it?" I interrupted. "Doesn't resemble anything I know."

"That's because this older nature spirit is a cross between a crocodile, a bush cow, and an antelope. The red paint symbolizes blood and danger. It's called a Goli Glin and represents older males. And since it's not considered as scary as the Bo Nun Amuin, the women and children can look at it, but they can't get too close."

"What about the bottom left?" I asked. "It gives me a feeling of innocence, and yet it's horned."

"You're on the right track there. The style represents young women. It's called a Kpan Pre."

I laughed and said, "So let me play genius here. The one on the bottom right with the elaborate coiffure has to represent older women, right?"

She nodded and teased, "So what's it called? You want to take a guess?"

"Ah, let's see. If the girl's mask is a Kpan *Pre*, then perhaps the woman's mask is a Kpan *Post*."

She laughed aloud and replied, "What is it you say all the time? Close but…"

"Close but no cigar!"

"That's right. So, yes, Jason, you're close but no cigar. You just drop the Pre off of Kpan Pre and then you've got it."

"Just Kpan then?'"

"That's right, just Kpan."

I walked over to one of the framed pictures and said, "Now you're playing in my ballpark. I know these lithographs and woodcuts like the back of my hand." I then did an immediate double take. "My God, Ivory! And they are all signed, too! That's 'Sky Castle.' Here's 'Convex and Concave.' That's 'Crab

Canon.' And over there, one of my all-time favorite Eschers, 'Cube with Magic Ribbons.' My God, where did you get them?"

She smiled and said, "On loan from an anonymous donor."

"Your parents again?"

"You got me! It's a small sample from my father's collection. These Eschers are very dear to him."

"You got to choose these?"

She nodded.

"And you chose them because they're included in *Gödel, Escher, Bach*?"

She nodded again.

"That's just unfu—That's just unreal!"

She slipped her arm up under mine, started guiding me gently toward the hallway, and declared, "You haven't seen anything yet!" When we reached the doorway leading to the rest of the apartment, Ivory stopped me and said, "Now close your eyes." She then steered me around the corner into the hallway, turned me to the right, and instructed me to open them again. I blinked several times and found myself standing in front of what appeared to be a small, framed note.

"What is it?" I asked.

"First, check the letterhead."

"It says, 'Institute for Advanced Studies, Princeton, New Jersey.'"

"Okay, and who's the recipient?"

"I don't know. It says, 'Dear E.'"

"I'll give you that one. It was my father's nickname while he was a visiting member of the AIS in 1970. 'E.' for Eboué. What does the rest say?"

"Ah… 'Would like your considered opinion. The proof's based on Leibniz's version of Saint Anselm.'"

"And the initials?"

"Hmm, looks like 'K.G.'"

"Any idea what you're looking at?"

I shrugged my shoulders.

"It's the cover note for a prized possession that my father keeps under lock and key."

"What's that?"

"The writer's ontological proof."

I leaned in, examined the initials more closely, and exclaimed, "No way! Your father knew Kurt Gödel?"

"Much more than that. My father *worked* with him for a year during his fellowship at AIS in Princeton and then corresponded with him almost to the end of Gödel's life."

"But I don't understand. I'd read Gödel developed his proof of God's existence in the early forties. So how does that square with Gödel asking your father to peer review his proof in 1970?"

"Father says Gödel had kept the work under wraps for years because he didn't want to get into an unproductive debate about whether he did or didn't believe in God. The only reason he circulated the draft to a few close associates in '70 was because he thought he was dying."

"He was something of a hypochondriac, wasn't he?"

She nodded and replied, "Yes, but father contends it was the paranoia that ravaged him."

"Paranoia? How? About what?"

"Gödel thought someone was trying to poison him. It got to the point where he would only eat food his wife had prepared. When she became ill and was hospitalized for going on six months, he stopped eating and died. The autopsy listed his weight at sixty-five pounds. The death certificate declared the cause of death as malnutrition and starvation caused by a personality disorder. So you could argue the paranoia indeed killed him."

"And to think that Einstein once confided to a colleague that he considered it a privilege to take daily walks with Gödel around Princeton. Oh, how the mighty have fallen. Just saying. It's food for thought."

Whenever Ivory sensed I was beginning to spin downward, she would find a way to lighten the atmosphere and haul me back up out of an impending funk. She pulled me in close and whispered, "Speaking of food… you getting hungry?"

I knew exactly what she was doing. So I smiled and said, "Luckily your scheme and my stomach agree. Let's eat!"

We continued down the hallway and entered a large kitchen/dining space divided visually by an island and four polished chrome barstools. But again, first things first. As she approached the stove, Ivory turned and said lightheartedly, "Why don't you take a safari: find the big cat and bring him back here to eat. I've kept his kidney and liver stew warming on the stove all this time."

I laughed and replied, "Amazing! Geb gets to eat before we do! What's up with that?"

"Once we get the big fellow watered and fed, we'll have the rest of the evening to share with each other. So hurry back now!" She poked my side playfully and we both laughed.

Ivory was good for her word. After lavishing considerable attention on the little upstage artist, she turned and said, "Just wait to see what we've got in store for you, big boy." She opened the refrigerator and began pulling out one casserole after another and carrying them over to the stove. "I've been working on our Ivorian buffet the past few days," she said. "I like to prepare the dishes in advance. It gives the flavors a chance to meld, you see."

Once everything was heated, we carried the dishes into the dining room, lined them up at the foot of the table, and piled our plates high with a little bit of everything. As we consumed our first helpings, I began asking questions about the various dishes. "This is absolutely delicious, Ivory. It has a wonderful sweet-salty flavor. What is it? How do you make it?"

"That's mafé, my father's favorite. It's a stew served over couscous or rice. I made this mafé here for you using my grandmother's special recipe. Let's see, it's got cubed beef, onion, garlic, ginger, tomatoes, and several cups of ground peanuts. Simmer for about an hour and you're all set."

"Well, it's delicious. And this?"

"Kedjenou. Another of my father's favorites. Another stew, but prepared a little differently. You put your chicken pieces, eggplant, tomatoes, onions, chili peppers, and spices in a well-sealed pot without any added water, and you bake it about three hours on a medium temperature. Now let me show you how to eat kedjenou. Put your fork down. See the ball of dough there?"

I nodded.

"Now take your fingers and tear off a piece of the dough, like this. Then shape it into a scoop and dip it into the kedjenou."

I gave it a try. "What's the dough?" I asked.

"Fufu. A mash of plantains or yams. I used yams for today."

"Everything's delicious. It's really interesting how you get such exotic flavors just by changing up the ingredients a bit.… Now what's this?" I pointed to a small platter of what appeared to be fried bananas with some kind of salad on the side.

"A side dish. Alloco. I learned to make Alloco years ago while helping my mother and grandmother with the meals. You fry up some plantains in palm oil, add some salt, and put a mixture of tomatoes, chili peppers, and onions on the plate alongside. It's a popular fast food. Find it all over Abidjan. But you find the best in the upscale district of Cocody. You'll see businessmen and ambassadors piling out of their mansions and queuing up like everyone else at their favorite vendors."

After biting into a large piece of the chili pepper, my throat began burning and my eyes watering. I looked around for something to drink.

"What do you need?" she asked.

I began waving my hand in front of my mouth and said, "The pepper's a little spicy. Something to put the fire out."

She rushed into the kitchen and returned with a small bowl of sugar and a large tumbler of water. "Here, take a pinch of this sugar first and then drink the water." Ivory paused as I dissolved the sugar in my mouth and then downed the whole glass of water. She then added apologetically, "Hey, I'm really sorry about the water. My family's custom is to drink water *after* the meal, not with it."

I laughed. "No problem, Ivory. Really, no problem at all. I'm ready for seconds now. How about you?"

While I helped myself to more mafé and kedjenou, Ivory disappeared into an adjoining room and flipped on the stereo. When she returned, she dimmed the overhead lights, lit two candles framing a floral centerpiece, pointed toward the other room, and said, "The music. Can you solve for *x*?"

"The Emerson," I teased.

"The work, silly."

"Ah… scored for keyboard but played here as a string quartet."

"The *work*?"

I continued the banter. "The quartet's far more transparent. Allows for a better sense of texture and balance of the contrapuntal line. The quartet's far easier on the ear than the harpsichord. Far more colorful than the piano."

She stood with her arms akimbo, smiled, and raised her voice, "Last chance now. *The work?*"

"Okay, okay. It's old Bach's last work, *Die Kunst der Fuge.* Like Mahler's *Tenth,* left unfinished at death. Ah, what did Bach's son write on the last page of the manuscript?"

"C.P.E. wrote, 'At the point where the composer introduces the name *BACH*'—you know, B♭–A–C–B♮—'in the counter-subject to this fugue, the composer died.' But I'm not buying it, Jason."

"Why's that?"

"The last pages are in Bach's hand, and they are very clean. They had to have been written sometime before his sight failed and his handwriting became practically illegible."

"But why would he leave the work unfinished like that? Doesn't make any sense."

"Of course it does. He left it for us."

"For us to complete?"

She shook her head. "For us to continue. He allows his loops to bottom out, so to speak. I'm convinced he left it for us to pick up his recursions and continue on."

"Got to hand it to you, Ivory, that's a fascinating idea. Trusting us mortals to carry on with his argument." I paused, cleared my throat, and said, "If you don't mind my asking…"

"What's that?"

"When we first met you said your father gave you a Bible and a copy of *Gödel, Escher, Bach* as gifts for your First Communion. The Bible makes sense, but Hofstadter?"

"Like Gödel, my father's religious. Our family's devout Catholic."

"So Gödel did believe in God?"

She nodded. "He confided to my father he didn't attend church but read the Bible every Sunday morning. Gödel explained he was a theist following in the footsteps of Leibniz."

"But why *GEB*?"

"My father believed if the Bible ever became passé for me, Hofstadter's insights would surely guide me back home. You know, Hofstadter's interpretation of Gödel's 'Incompleteness Theorem,' from meaningless symbols to a self-referencing statement: '*I* exist but *I* am not provable.'"

"In a sense your father was borrowing from the Jesuits' playbook. You know, teaching students calculus, reasoning if they fully grasped the concepts of the infinite, the students would then have a better understanding of God."

"Exactly."

"Curious. Did your father ever try drawing parallels between the two—between the Bible and *GEB*?"

"Yes, and I'll never forget," she said. "When I was going on twelve, I asked him if he had a favorite Bible verse. He said he did. From the New Testament, the Book of John. The first verse of the first chapter."

"What does it say?"

"'In the beginning was the Word, and the Word was with God, and the Word was God.'"

"I wonder why it was his favorite."

"He explained it was a unique glimpse before the big bang, before Genesis begins. A glance at the meaningless primitives roiling in a primordial stew. 'In the beginning was the Word.'"

"So 'the Word' represents the meaningless primitives?"

"That's right. Next we have the big bang, 'and the Word was with God.'"

"So the meaningless primitives are taking on meaning now, in the process of *becoming* God?"

"Yes. And the verse ends, 'and the Word *was* God.'"

"I understand, but Hofstadter emphasizes the self-referencing."

"Father had an answer for that too. He said his second favorite passage was the beginning of the book of Genesis. 'In the beginning God created the heavens and the earth. And the earth was without form and void; and darkness was upon the face of the deep. And the Spirit of God moved upon the face of the waters. And God said, "Let there be light; and there was light."' He explained it didn't take long for the self-referencing to begin. *I* say, 'Let there be light.' It only takes three verses in Genesis before a self appears out of things that have no selves."

I smiled and nodded. "Yeah, I get it. From axiom to string to proof. Meaning from meaninglessness, an 'I' from a 'non-I,' cleverly overlaying Hofstadter's fugue on the books of Genesis and John."

As Bach's Contrapuctus 9 transitioned from a galloping D minor to a soaring D major chord, we moved over to the sofa where I lay my head on Ivory's lap and stretched my legs out across the cushions. I stared up into her smile and asked, "Do you think this was all predetermined?"

She stroked my hair gently and asked, "What's that, Jason?"

"Our meeting. You and me. Following Hofstadter's premise, from axiom to proof, from nothingness to everything. After my friends abandoned the house, leaving me alone, I have to admit I was drifting. As your father would say I had regressed to 'a meaningless primitive roiling in primordial stew.' But then, from an invisible voice beneath me all the way to this? A growing relationship distilling the meaning out of meaninglessness. Your willingness to roll with the punches, to take me at face value, the way I am, not the way you might want or expect me to be."

"My philosophy professor would call that 'causal determinism,' accepting the universe as a formal system operating deterministically. I don't know if I can buy it. After all, where does free will fit in to all of this?"

"Well, you have to at least consider Laplace's demon."

"Laplace's demon?" she asked.

"Yeah. Boiling it down, Laplace suggested if you were to give him the position and momentum of every particle in the universe at its inception, he could accurately predict the future. Everything had been set in motion at the beginning."

She shook her head. "Sounds too much like a program spinning out fractals. Reminds me of *The Matrix*."

As I continued gazing up into her eyes, I unleashed a silent rejoinder: "I'm stymied, Ivory. I can't roll out the big guns supporting the argument without violating my clearance. But believe me, there were precursors, relationships, true primitives, which have only now taken on meaning. The guidance counselor, Mrs. Prescott, shaping the Poker Flats Social Club. The special ed teacher, Ms. Davis, suggesting personal computers for our homes. Our fifth-grade taskmaster, Mrs. Summerfield, introducing us to *The Oregon Trail*. Bones suggesting a declaration of independence. Zu's unfailing courage to act. Stats hacking and helping plug the myriad holes in Thunderwood 7.0. Special Agent Beale ordering cable construction. Geb running up a tree, which brings us up to your invisible voice ringing out beneath me on that special day."

Ivory continued stroking my hair and tried breaking my silence. "A penny for your thoughts."

I shrugged.

"You okay, Jason?" she asked.

I nodded.

And as the final notes of Bach's chorale resolved in harmony, Ivory lifted me up onto her breast and rocked me gently in the soft, warm mercy of her means.

20

A FTER THE CONTRACTORS COMPLETED the basement buildout, I spent the next six months laboring in the belly of the beast. But to be totally honest, it wasn't as bad as I let on. The contractors had actually converted the unfinished basement into a comfortable apartment with a walled-off bedroom, a kitchen/dining area, a private bath, and a generous workspace. And these first six months in the catacombs admittedly flew by fast. They were devoted 24/7 to enhancing Thunderwood 7.0, installing telephones and computer clusters, and ensuring all the computer and telecommunication links had been established, secured, and thoroughly tested.

From the project's launch until now, Special Agent Beale had held update meetings every Monday morning at eight o'clock sharp. Because of his leadership style, there was a strong esprit de corps, and individual morale remained consistently high. He managed to take politics and rivalry out of the project on day one. While chewing on an unlit cigar, he said, "When an issue crops up, I don't want to know who did it. I just want to know how long it's going to take you to get it fixed." So there were never any games of "gotcha." Everyone pitched in to work a problem even when it wasn't officially on our respective plates.

The update meeting that morning promised to be memorable. We would begin transitioning from the centralized implementation and pilot-testing phase to a nationwide rollout. In fact, we were so excited to finally get under way that Thomas, Rich, Henry, and I gathered around the table in the first-floor dining area at fifteen minutes of eight. And I believe Special Agent Beale was tuned in to the same wavelength. He strolled into the meeting only five minutes later, when he usually rounded the corner as the clock chimed eight.

He thumbed through his massive project folder, located a freshly updated Gantt chart, and said, "Okay. First I'll give you a brief update on activities back East. The good news is the volume and intensity of chatter about the grid have remained relatively low, which buys us a little more time to work out the kinks here. The bad news is the analysts as yet haven't managed to pin down the likely targets for potential physical attacks. They've emphasized on several occasions they still believe these strikes on substations will most likely be limited and diversionary in nature but feel that our knowing the targeted locations might help us better prepare to defend the control center systems.

"Any questions so far about activities back East?" He looked at each of us. "None? Okay. So let's talk about our status here. According to the work plan, Rich, you and Henry have finished coding and beta testing the offensive module. Correct?"

Rich nodded. "Correct. And the next step is to work with Jason and Henry to integrate our module into the master copy of Thunderwood we have running here."

"And your drop-dead date for getting that done?"

Rich looked over at me and asked, "What do you think, Jason? A month?"

I nodded and answered, "Yeah, that's fair."

"Okay, a month it is," Special Agent Beale said as he posted the date on his chart to emphasize a contractlike commitment to honor the target date. "So, Jason, how close are you and Henry to finishing the centralized detection module?"

"It's fully tested and integrated into the master software here. And once copies of Thunderwood have been uploaded and are running at the various control centers, we can then test the handshakes between our central system and their databases out there."

The agent jumped in. "Which reminds me, Jason. IT back East said they will start loading Thunderwood onto the local control center systems next Monday and begin testing. They've also committed to a two-week turnaround for a nationwide implementation. So given that timeline, Jason, how long will you and Henry need to fully test the links and ensure the local detection tools are working and talking to our master copy back here?"

I looked over at Henry and asked, "What do you think? Two weeks?"

Henry shook his head, gritted his teeth, and replied, "Ah, you better go with three, Jason. If it doesn't work as advertised, it's a show stopper."

Special Agent Beale put ink to paper and said, "So your drop-dead date is three weeks from today, correct?"

We nodded and answered, "Yes, sir."

"Okay. Are there any questions? Anyone?" The five of us looked at each other. "Well, let's get back to work and finish this phase of the mission. What do you say?"

We all stood up and responded, "Yes, sir!" before going our separate ways.

There is an old battlefield adage that states, "War is long periods of boredom punctuated by moments of sheer terror." As I quickly learned, state-sponsored attacks are low in profile and slow in the making. I gradually grew to think of myself as a sniper waiting and watching for a chance to pounce. But after months of continuous monitoring without the slightest hint of a breach anywhere along the grid, I was beginning to question the honeypot I had created to lure cyberterrorists into our virtual onsite systems. My goal was to walk a fine line between making the vulnerability too obvious, where hackers would sense something was up, and too hidden, where it might remain undiscovered for months or even years.

But just as I was about to acknowledge a screwup, the overnight scan produced a possible breach in the eastern interconnection at a control center northeast of Birmingham. A surge of adrenaline rushed through me, not because the alert was there but because I came so close to missing it. I had gotten so used to scanning the reports and finding nothing that the flag buried near the end of the multiscreen display almost failed to register in my numbed brain. I did a double take. At first I thought I was seeing things. I swung around in my chair and raced up the stairs, shouting, "An exploit! A breach!" And everyone and his brother followed the pied piper down cellar to share in the thrill of our initial success.

After surveying the online report, Special Agent Beale turned and said, "Link us up to Birmingham's virtual system, Jason, and project it onto the big screen so we can all have a look."

"Sure thing, Brian!" I said eagerly.

He then turned to Rich and said, "When Jason's got us in, sit down there and run the packets through the scanner. See what we're dealing with. If it's other than old hat or variance, activate the debugger module and get on it right away. You'll have some real fun reverse engineering line by line if it's something entirely new."

Rich nodded, cracked his knuckles, and smiled, as if telegraphing his prayer that the malware was indeed entirely new. But that wasn't surprising. I remembered an earlier conversation where he rhapsodized about how much he relished the thrill of "scratching and clawing" his way through line after line of assembly and then reveling in the artful coding of malicious genius.

When the database appeared on the projection screen, I jumped up and motioned for Rich to take a seat. As he began keying in commands, he asked, "Say, Jason, the scanner's current, right?"

"Sure is," I replied. "I updated it yesterday, late afternoon."

And after running several scans just to be sure, Rich, sounding like he'd just won the lottery, announced, "Well, gentlemen, it appears the boys overseas have given us a truly unique gift. It looks like we're dealing with something entirely new."

Special Agent Beale took a long, slow drag on his cigar and said, "Well then, Rich, do whatever it takes to crack the shell."

"Yes, sir!" Rich replied.

The agent moved toward the stairs, looked back over his shoulder, and counterintuitively tried lightening up the load by raising the stakes. "And Rich," he added.

"Yes, sir?"

"No pressure now, you hear? But make it quick. Your job and the country's future are riding on it."

Rich smiled at the compliment and quoted Foch at the First Battle of the Marne: "My center's yielding. My right's retreating. Situation excellent. I'm attacking!"

And attack he did. At the end of a long month Rich convened a weekend meeting to deliver his findings. "Well, first out of the box, I've got to tell you this ain't your mother's Stuxnet. It has some similarities, but we're dealing with some really sophisticated shit here."

"How are they different?" Special Agent Beale asked.

"It's much bigger than Stuxnet. I estimate eighty times bigger. It's huge! Five hundred kilobytes versus forty frigging megabytes."

The rest of us mumbled some variant of "Jesus Christ!"

Rich explained, "The exploit monitors the host and steals data either through packet sniffing or keystroke monitoring. Appears to have backdoor functionality for updates and emergency self-destruct commands. There are a number of levels of encryption and at least twenty-five modules and plug-ins, which can be shuffled in and out to further customize functionality."

He paused and looked over at me. "A word of warning to you, Jason. I'm telling you, this is really gnarly stuff. It can turn on internal microphones to capture conversations and take screenshots of your emails and instant messaging. Before you know it, one of their boys will be downloading your info off a command and control server. So caution's the word when you're scouting about in the virtual systems. Got it?"

"Thanks, Rich! Got it! We'll just have to figure out a workaround."

"So the bottom line here is we're not dealing with yokels. The software's too advanced for that. This has to be state sponsored; and it's my guess this is the prelude to an all-out attack on the grid."

Not long after that weekend meeting, I watched the battlefield begin taking shape right before my eyes. First there were exploits in the Texas Interconnection—control centers outside San Antonio, Houston, Dallas, and Austin. Next we had breaches in the Western Interconnection—control centers near Portland, Los Angeles, Denver, and Phoenix. And finally there were additional intrusions into the eastern interconnection—control centers outside Albany, Philadelphia, and Chicago.

Over the next six weeks I kept a close eye on all the malware lurking about within the breached virtual systems. The behavior was consistent among all the exploits. At that point the malware's mission appeared to be solely data gathering. There were no offensive modules attached and no indication a cyberattack was imminent. I watched daily as the malware captured the phony data in the virtual systems and transmitted it back to four staging areas scattered about the United States. These intermediate stops (i.e., compromised domestic websites) were designed primarily to cover the terrorists' tracks. They planned storing these data at the staging points for some period of time before moving them over to their computers somewhere, we suspected, in Eastern Europe.

When we held our regularly scheduled update meeting, Special Agent Beale said, "Thanks to Jason's hard work, we now have a pretty good idea where the attacks will occur, but we still don't know when. Any ideas?"

I raised my hand. "I've had a lot of time to think about that while hanging out downstairs monitoring the breaches," I said. "One possible scenario: I've looked at their important dates and holidays. I've looked at ours. But I keep coming back to a hunch

I had early on. I believe they're going to be more practical this time than focusing on a meaningful date."

"Practical?" the agent asked.

I nodded. "Yes. Why not attack when the grid's most vulnerable?"

"And when's that?" Rich asked.

"When it's under maximum stress. The last week or two of July, maybe the first week in August. That way they get the most leverage, the most bang for their buck with the fewest number of exploits and the fewest chances for detection. Let the grid, so to speak, help in its own demise."

"Not bad thinking, Jason. Not bad at all."

"One more thing, ah… Brian."

"What's that?"

"Now it might be a stretch, but I also got to thinking.… I know the boys back East believe any attacks on physical assets— big substation transformers, transmission lines, and the like— will most likely be head fakes. But what if they aren't? What if saboteurs do go after critical transformers for real? And to top it off, what if they went after the few transformer manufacturers we have in the country. I looked it up. There are only a handful. If the terrorists took out critical transformers and then the factories building replacements, the country could be without power for two years or more. So, just saying, if the boys back East aren't already working this angle, I think they should at least give it some thought."

The agent gazed into my eyes, shook his head incredulously, and said, "I'll be sure someone's looking into the factories right away."

242

21

S PECIAL AGENT BEALE RACED down the stairs into the command center and asked, "Anything happening with the malware?"

I shook my head. "No. Steady as she goes. Why you asking?"

"I just got an urgent email from Headquarters. There's been an attack overnight on a large substation southwest of Kansas City. Overland Park, just off Interstate 35."

"Jesus!"

"You're sure no assault modules have been loaded into the malware, correct?"

"Stake my life on it, Brian. Everything's the same. This is probably a dress rehearsal of what the boys back East are calling the head fake. But tell me, what happened?"

"From what they've been able to piece together so far, the assault started at about one o'clock a.m. local. Opened several manhole covers near the substation, climbed down into an underground bunker, and cut critical fiber-optic cables disabling telephone, Internet, and emergency 911 service. The saboteurs then proceeded to the substation where a surveillance camera detected a brief flash of light, probably a signal to commence firing. Next, the video picked up muzzle flashes and sparks from bullets hitting metal. And finally the camera detected a second flash of light, probably a signal to cease fire. And that was at about one fifty a.m."

"Cameras capture any pictures of the gunmen?"

"No. The cameras were aimed along the chain-link fences, not outside the substation perimeter."

"Anybody hear anything?"

"A truck driver passing by on I-35 called the police and reported gunfire. This was well into the assault, just about when the shooting stopped."

"Any motion detectors there?"

"Sure, but they didn't sound the alarm until late in the game. Probably stray bullets ricocheting inside the compound set them off."

"Any of the transformers crash?"

"All told, twenty of them."

"That must have set off failure alarms at the control center monitoring that particular area."

"It did. And the only good news about all this is the operators were able to reroute power around the Overland Park substation and get local plants to increase production. They did a good job keeping the suburbs up and running."

"The police find anything when they got there?"

"A locked fence and a couple hundred shell casings consistent with AK-47s.

There's a wide gravel bed just outside the chain-link fence. That's where they were standing to fire into the rows of transformers some fifty yards away. Didn't miss a target either. Must have had night vision scopes mounted on their weapons."

"Strange that nothing blew."

"These weren't some local dudes hopped up on brewskies or meth. These were terrorists executing a well-planned attack full stop! They didn't fire directly at the transformers themselves and risk explosions. No. They aimed at the oil-filled cooling systems. Riddled them with holes, causing thousands of gallons of oil to spill out into the compound."

"So instead of exploding they overheated and shut down?"

"You got it. Clever, huh?"

"Any clues inside the substation?"

He nodded. "Yes. That's the weirdest thing of all. The police said they found gravel piled up on the twenty or so transformers that the saboteurs targeted. Remember now, the gates were locked."

"Inside job?"

"Perhaps. But time will tell. They're assigning the boys from the Joint Warfare Analysis Center in Virginia to try to unravel this." He paused, stared directly into my eyes, and said, "What this tells me, Jason, is that we're dealing with the crème de la crème. So you're one hundred percent sure nothing's going on with the malware? No offensive modules being loaded on? Nothing like that?"

"I'm telling you, nothing's happening right now. I check the reports daily and monitor each of the targeted systems several times a day. There's nothing going on."

"I just want to make sure when they do load on the attack modules, you capture a copy so we can analyze the hell out of it. You know, protect the country for the future."

I nodded and said, "Yeah, I know, Brian."

"And one other thing I want you to do once they've loaded the attack modules on. I want you to blow the hell out of those four staging points in the States. I know their systems in Eastern Europe are still a bridge too far, but obliterating those hijacked websites here in the US will set the bastards back several years."

"Yes, sir!" I shouted. "Believe me, I look forward to pulling the trigger and watching those mothers disintegrate."

"Well, carry on, Jason. And remember now, no pressure. But the country's counting on you to finish the bastards off." He smiled, turned, and then climbed the stairs in long, powerful strides.

22

IT WAS LATE JULY. I was hanging out with Ivory at her place on her birthday when a text message from Rich appeared on my phone: "Please pick up some milk on your way home." After responding, "Roger. Copy," I pushed back from the kitchen table and said, "I can't explain right now, Ivory, but a friend's in trouble and I have to go bail him out."

Ivory looked at me with concern. "What's wrong? Can I go with you?"

"Uh, no. That's not going to work. I'm sorry. I know it's your birthday and everything, but I really do have to go."

"Well, okay. Call me later then." I could hear the disappointment in her voice.

"Listen, I'll drop by later on to explain, okay? I mean when everything's settled down. Sound good?" She nodded. I kissed her forehead and said, "I love you," then headed for the door.

I raced back to Headquarters and immediately sensed the mood had shifted since I had left less than two hours before. The relaxed banter had been replaced with tense silence; the laughter with serious game faces. Special Agent Beale was on his cell. When he saw me enter, he raised his hand, signaling I should stop and wait until he had finished his conversation. In the meantime, I scanned the room. It was humming. Everyone had his face buried in a manual or glued to a laptop monitor.

When the agent ended his call, he approached and said, "The thunder's beginning to roll in, Jason."

"Yeah, I suspected as much. I got Rich's text and came right back. Where is he? Downstairs?"

Beale nodded. "Yes. He was monitoring the situation until you could get back and take over."

"So what's up?" I tossed my keys on the table and hung up my beret.

"Rich says they're loading something new on the malware. He suspects it's the offensive module."

"One locale or more?" I asked.

"So far, just Birmingham, where we saw the first intrusion."

"What about the physical assets? Any movement on that front?"

The agent shook his head and said, "That's who I was talking to just now. The boys back East are running around with their hair on fire. Never have been able to pin down any potential targets. No chatter whatsoever about the substations or transmission lines. When I passed along the news just now about Birmingham, they went ballistic, excoriating the assets and the analysts for not coming up with something. They're afraid the saboteurs will launch four or five of these head fakes, do a lot of damage. And they don't have actionable intelligence to perhaps blunt the attacks while giving us clues to the possible sequencing of events in our cyber war here." He paused and gazed into my eyes. "You ready to take the side-stick?"

"Yes, sir, and if you don't mind, I'd prefer flying this single-seat Raptor alone. No distractions downstairs. Prefer keeping everyone out of the command center. Communicate by text if necessary. Y'all have the same computer cluster upstairs in my old bedroom as I have downstairs. Y'all can see everything that's going on in real time. So you okay with a single-seater?"

"Fair enough—as long as you keep us posted about anomalies you're finding along the way."

I extended my hand and said, "It's a deal. I'll send Rich right up."

"By the way, how you doing for rations down there?" he asked.

I smiled and replied, "I stock the fridge with favorites every Friday morning, and today was no exception. I'm loaded for bear."

He patted me on the shoulder and said, "Godspeed, Jason."

"Thank you, sir. And if you get an update on potential physical attacks, fire off a text to me."

"Consider it done."

I turned, and as I moved toward the cellar door, a bolt of lightning flashed across an angry sky, announcing the arrival of a strong afternoon storm.

Following a debrief on the Birmingham system, I escorted Rich to the first-floor landing, assured him everything was going to be just fine, and locked the door once he disappeared around the corner. I descended into the gloom, lit half a dozen candles, and moved over to my legacy videocassette recorder. I fast-forwarded the tape until the counter read "653" and then hit play:

> *Well, we're way past big speech time. I want to thank you for the last few months. It's been very special for me. Anybody have anything they want to say?*

> *Yeah. Let's win this one for all the small schools that never had a chance to get here.*

I switched off the VCR, sat down at the console, and keyed in the codes activating Thunderwood's counterattack module for the first time in combat.

For the next thirty-six hours I kept my finger close to the trigger as I watched the bastards methodically upload attack modules one after another onto the control center systems: Albany, Philadelphia, Chicago, San Antonio, Houston, Dallas, Austin. And finally, in the wee hours of Sunday morning: Portland, Los Angeles, Denver, and Phoenix. I tracked their feedback packets moving from our software back to the staging points, confirming their attack modules had been successfully installed and armed. The hacked website portals were now wide open.

With my finger hovering above the return key, I whispered, "'With God of heaven, it is all one: To deliver with a great multitude, or a small company. For the victory of battle standeth not in the multitude of hosts, but strength cometh from heaven. And David put his hand in the bag and took out a stone and slung it, and struck the Philistine on the head, and he fell to the ground.'" I took a deep breath, lowered my hand onto the keyboard, and launched four offensive packets toward the saboteurs' lairs.

Several minutes later I tried logging on to each of the hijacked websites. I smiled. There was nothing left but cyber ash. Thunderwood had worked flawlessly. The staging points were fried. I retreated to my subterranean bedroom, sat down on the edge of the bed, and buried my head in my hands.

23

W HEN MY CELL ON the nightstand vibrated, I reluctantly picked it up and read Special Agent Beale's text message: "When does the guest of honor plan on gracing us with his presence? It's getting pretty wild up here. ;)"

I could tell. It had been less than an hour since the counter-attack, and I could hear the laughter, the music, and the women's voices. I responded: "Just as soon as I can shower, shave, and find something appropriate for the occasion."

After showering I sat down at the vanity in my room, stared into the mirror, and said, "So, Geb, what do you think? Too much blush? How about the brows? The mascara and shadow? Has to be subtle, you know. Not too much. Otherwise, what would people think?"

I stared into his beautiful green eyes, stroked his chin, and asked, "What about the jewelry?… Yeah, I was leaning that way too. The sterling cross necklace and earrings. After all, it's the first day of the week, and I know it's hard hearing the bells over the din upstairs. And what should I be today? Blond or brunette? Brunette? Very well then, brunette it will be."

I moved over to the closet, pulled out a dress and a pantsuit from the far end of the rack, and held both up against my chest. "So which one, Geb? The yellow sleeveless fit-and-flare or the white-and-beige pinstriped suit? I agree—the pantsuit it is! 'And what about the shoes?' you ask. I think we better go with these closed-toe flats. How about you? Very good then." I sat back down at the mirror for a final look, lightly brushed my hair, and asked, "You ready to go see Ivory? You are? Okay, then, big boy, let's get going." I rubbed noses with the kitty, picked him up, and climbed to the top of the stairs.

When I reached the landing, I stopped and listened to the loud screams and laughter reverberating just beyond the door. I could feel my heart pounding as I slowly turned the key in the knob, pushed the door open, and stepped out into the room. Within seconds the celebratory bedlam became gasps and then a deafening silence. Host and guest alike stepped back, forming a wall of bewilderment to our left and right, as Geb and I began moving through their tunnel toward the front door. Floyd was right; the path to heaven does indeed run through miles of clouded hell.

I gently stowed Geb under my arm and stepped out onto the porch. I took several deep breaths of the warm, fresh Sunday morning air. I descended the stairs and followed the familiar path out onto Jackson Avenue. Everything was the same as it had been on every other Sunday morning, when I made quick runs downtown to the coffee shop. And admittedly, the sameness today was both soothing and reassuring—the same chirping, the same barking, the same chimes, the same aromatic bacon frying, the same cop waving, the same family waiting, the same siren wailing, the same music blaring, and the same freight rumbling through our waking town.

I stepped into the shop, grabbed a rare, voluminous Sunday *Times*, and fell in behind the tenth devotee in line. When it was finally my turn, the young barista smiled and asked, "What can I get you, ma'am?"

I had an almost irresistible urge to laugh but managed to limit the joyous impulse to a smile. I replied, "Make it two large lattes and a couple of cheese Danish to go." As the barista foamed the milk I asked, "Anything big going on in the news today?"

He answered, "Same old, same old. It's been pretty boring all summer if you ask me."

"Sometimes boring's good. I had to learn that along the way."

"That'll be six bucks."

"Here's a ten. Put the change in the kitty."

"Thank you, ma'am, and have a great day."

I smiled and replied, "I'm sure gonna try."

As I neared Ivory's apartment complex, I stopped in a small neighborhood park, sat down, and scanned the front page of the *Times*. I wanted to sense what *their* success felt and looked like. And there it was, blaring out of the headlines: "Rebellion in the Ukraine" and "E-Cigarettes Deliver Toxins." No bulletins about terrorism, blackouts, or the grid.

I climbed the stairs to Ivory's second-floor apartment, rang the bell, and waited anxiously for judgment day. When she opened the door, there was only the slightest pause to absorb and recalibrate before she said, "Let's see now. We have Geb, Jason, and fresh-brewed coffee. By all means, come in. You've made my day!" But of course, the upstage artist was at it again. Ivory eased Geb out from under my arm, rubbed noses with him, and asked, "You hungry, big boy? Well, I've got something special for you this fine Sunday morning—a piece of grilled salmon left over from last night. What do you say?" As usual, she turned and motioned for *me* to follow *them* into the kitchen. She broke up the large piece of fish, warmed it in the microwave, and parked Geb and his feast beneath the table.

She then turned, extended her arms, and pulled me in close. After a long, accepting embrace, she held me out at arm's length and said, "I believe the Greek's come bearing gifts."

I opened the bag and replied, "A token of penitence for leaving you alone on your birthday the other night. Your favorite, lattes and cheese Danish."

Ivory smiled mischievously, poured our lattes into ceramic cups, took a bite out of each of the pastries, and said, "There, that's the price you've had to pay for rushing out!" We moved into the living room, sat down on the sofa, and chatted about this and that until we had finished our drinks and Danish. She then tapped lightly on her lap, signaling I should lie down and stretch out across the cushions. I lay down, closed my eyes, and asked myself, "Okay, then, what now?" And I recalled asking the same question when Special Agent Beale and I struck a devil's bargain: in exchange for my software and expertise the government wouldn't press charges against the unsuspecting Stats, Bones, Zulu, and me. I remembered that demanding smile as he described the deal as a "zero-sum game."

Ivory stroked my cheek with the back of her hand and teased, "A nickel for your thoughts. How can you resist? That's a five hundred percent increase over my last offer."

I made an effort to smile and said, "Ah, I was just thinking about my old roommates. It's funny, here we are now with graduation barely in the rearview mirror, and all three of them have already landed jobs and are moving on."

"That's not unusual for Pantheon graduates."

"But what are the odds that they would all end up in the same city?"

"Where's that?" She asked.

"Washington."

"State?"

"No, DC."

Ivory remained genuinely engaged and asked, "So what are they up to?"

"You know Stats has always been into mathematics and sports. I suspected he would end up working for a sports network or a major league baseball or football team. But he's moving to Washington to get involved in a true blood sport."

"Blood sport?"

"Politics. Working on campaigns and writing a blog predicting congressional and presidential outcomes. His girlfriend—you've met Bones—she's going along too. She's always been fascinated with the sciences—anatomy, genetics, biology. She's landed a job working on an extension of the genome project, pursuing her theory about a second hidden genome."

"Fascinating."

"And Brenda—Zulu—she went to Saint Petersburg to study Russian history for a year but fell in love with contemporary Russian theater instead. Since she no longer has any reason to stay here now that her father's died, she's joining a well-respected repertory as a dramaturg advocating for more plays from Moscow's 'Theater of Pain.'"

"Your friends… they all sound like really interesting. People I'd like to get to know."

I nodded and said wistfully, "But unfortunately, they're going. Leaving me here alo——. It's hard. We grew up together, supported each other, found the gritty determination to exist, to carry on, to be. Whenever I would get really down, Bones would wrap her arm around my shoulder and softly sing lyrics from some twelfth-century hymn she'd found while doing research on an English project:

Quis rex, quae curia, quale palatium,
quae pax, quae requies, quod illud gaudium,
huius participes exponant gloriae,
si quantum sentiunt, possint exprimere.

Nostrum est interim mentem erigere
et totis patriam votis appetere,
et ad Ierusalem a Babylonia
post longa regredi tandem exsilia.

"What does it mean?"

"It's Latin. Something to the effect that in heaven there won't be a separation between wish and fulfillment, that all prayers will be answered. But in the meantime we just have to soldier on."

"Yes—that is, until we reclaim the dreams we lost in youth. Until we find the courage again *to become* rather than merely *to be*. It sounds like your friends have broken through and are becoming. So that leaves you, Jason. What now?"

"I honestly don't know, Ivory. I've been playing the black keys all my life."

She pushed back gently, "And I've been playing the white keys with my accent, heritage, and color?"

I nodded. "In our strange loop? Yes. I, the black, and you, the white."

She smiled and extended the metaphor. "So what kind of music are we going to write today, Mr. Bach? A passion? A fugue? You do seem to have a penchant for the minor key."

I shrugged my shoulders and answered seriously, "For some time now I've been a stranger in a strange land, where success is measured through a prism of anonymity and the status quo. Where fame is deadly and incidents are failures. I'm beginning to think the best is already behind me. That I'm on the downward arc. That I've done what I was put here to do."

She shook her head and said caringly, "Shame on you, Jason. You're always thinking in shades of blue and gray. You have to step out from the shadows and into the light."

And now it was my turn to object. "But I've been to the end of the rainbow, Ivory, and I'm telling you, I didn't find that pot of gold everyone promises is waiting for us there."

She smiled and said, "That's because you never reached the end."

"What do you mean?" I asked.

"You couldn't have. Step beyond the horizon, Jason, and you'll see. The rainbow's a circle. Your descending arc is but the foothills of the next climb." She then gently lifted my head up onto her breast, leaned in, and kissed me passionately.